DARK WATER RISING

DARK WATER RISING

Marian Hale

HENRY HOLT AND COMPANY

NEW YORK

Henry Holt and Company, LLC
Publishers since 1866
175 Fifth Avenue
New York, New York 10010
www.henryholtchildrensbooks.com

Photo credits: p. 222, courtesy of TXGenWEB's Texas Postcards (www.rootsweb.com/~txpst-crd); pp. 224, 225, 227, courtesy of NOAA; pp. 226, 228, 230, 232, courtesy of the Library of Congress; p. 229, photo by W. A. Green, courtesy of the Library of Congress.

Library of Congress Cataloging-in-Publication Data
Hale, Marian.
Dark water rising / Marian Hale.—1st ed.
p.   cm.
Summary: While salvaging and rebuilding in the aftermath of the Galveston flood of 1900, sixteen-year-old Seth proves himself in a way that his previous efforts never could, but he still must face his father man to man.
ISBN-13: 978-0-8050-7585-4
ISBN-10: 0-8050-7585-2
1. Hurricanes—Texas—Galveston—Juvenile fiction. [1. Hurricanes—Texas—Galveston—Fiction. 2. Fathers and sons—Fiction. 3. Family life—Texas—Fiction.
4. Race relations—Fiction. 5. Carpentry—Fiction. 6. Galveston (Tex.)—History—20th century—Fiction.] I. Title.
PZ7.H1373Dar 2006   [Fic]—dc22   2005036678

First Edition—2006
Book designed by Debora Smith
Printed in the United States of America on acid-free paper. ∞

10 9 8 7 6 5 4 3 2 1

For my husband,
Wendel,
my safe harbor

And for all those
who suffered the Great Storm
with no safe harbor

Chapter

1

The train clicked on its rails, rumbling past cow pastures and summer-parched fields of grain and hay. Open windows funneled dust and straw into my face, and all around me, sweaty children whined their discomfort. Mamas dug into bundles for crackers and cheese, bread and jam—anything to distract their little varmints from the sticky heat. I glanced around the crowded train car. You'd think every dang person from Lampasas to Houston wanted to go to Galveston this hot August day.

Everyone but me.

I shifted under the sleeping weight of four-year-old Kate, limp and sweaty in my lap, and dark curls fell across her face. Seems I couldn't breathe twice anymore without Mama saying, "Seth, would you button Kate's shoes for me?" or "Quick, Seth! Wipe that runny nose." And every blasted time Mama's hands were white with flour, she'd holler, "Seth, you'll have to take

Kate to the outhouse for me while I finish the bread." Just thinking of it got my dander up. Why God couldn't have sent that child just one big sister instead of three brothers was beyond my understanding.

Across from me, Matt's heat-red face puckered in a deep frown. He elbowed Lucas for more room, and when he didn't get it, he delivered a swift boot to the leg. I returned the kick before Lucas could even open his mouth to complain.

"You're twelve years old," I hissed at Matt. "Act like it."

He glanced across the aisle at Mama and Papa, making sure they hadn't seen, then turned back to me with a sneer. "Where's your apron, Seth?" he whispered. "If you're gonna sound like Mama, you oughta look like her, too." He nudged Lucas again. "Besides, you can take it, can't ya, Big Luke?"

Lucas shrugged. He rarely let Matt pull him into disagreements, but recently things had changed. He'd shot up so much this summer, it was impossible to tell who was taller. At just ten, his new height had become a sore spot with Matt, sparking some ornery mischief. Most of the time I ignored it, but today was different.

The train sped toward a spindly trestle strung across Galveston Bay and rumbled onto a fragile network of pilings and rails. Mama stiffened and reached for Papa's hand. I glanced out the windows at the green water all around and felt a bit like a kite flying too close to the waves, dragged toward the long, narrow island that was sure to be my undoing. And it was all my uncle's fault.

"Galveston is fast becoming the New York City of Texas," Uncle Nate had told Papa just two short weeks ago. "It's the third richest city in the country by population. We have electric lights, electric streetcars, local and long-distance telephone service, and three big concert halls."

I peered at the miles of wharves ahead, crowded with steamships, schooners, and fishing boats, and beyond the forest of masts, I saw three tremendous grain elevators.

"Twelve hundred ships load and unload cargo there every year," Uncle Nate had been quick to add. More proof, I supposed, that Galveston was *the* booming city of the new twentieth century.

It was true my uncle's lumber business had done well, but Uncle Nate thought Galveston could improve his younger brother's lot in life, too. I'd watched him that day through the porch windows, spouting his case for moving like some highfalutin Philadelphia lawyer.

"The 1900 census is projected to be better than thirty-seven thousand," he'd said, punctuating his words with a chewed cigar, "and all those people need houses, stores, and offices. There's big money to be made there, Thomas. That foreman job could open the door to your own contracting business."

At that point, Papa hadn't said a word, nor had his eyes registered an opinion either way, which had given me hope. He was a good carpenter, one of the best at Calloway and Sons, a company I planned to apprentice with as soon as my schooling was out of the way.

"Remember," Uncle Nate had continued, "Seth is almost seventeen. Time to settle his future."

I waited for Papa's answer, but he'd always been slow to share his mind and slower still to change it. As the seconds ticked away, Uncle Nate's face took on color. He flushed deep red and let loose with "Hellfire, Thomas!"

I jumped, almost giving away my position on the porch.

"The first medical college in Texas is right there in Galveston!" he bellowed. "Take the bloody position and send *all* your boys to college!"

That last statement set up a fierce flutter inside me. Papa already knew that working under a blue sky, shaping raw lumber into walls and doors, roofs and staircases, was all I'd ever wanted. But he'd also been clear about what *he* wanted for his sons. If he thought Galveston could ensure any of us a profession in medicine, we'd be on the next train out of Lampasas for sure.

I'd likely end up spending years poring over books and cadavers, and the rest of my life shut up inside a small white room, patching up boils and broken arms. The probability of that happening squirmed inside me like a bellyful of grub worms.

Uncle Nate poked his cigar between his teeth and gave Papa a lopsided grin. "I can get you a nice furnished rental close to the beach. You know how much Eliza and the kids would love that."

Mama *would* love that. I held my breath while the vacant expression on Papa's weathered face shifted. I saw a small glimmer of excitement, but it was the hunger in his eyes that finally made me clench my teeth with dread, the same kind of hunger that had always sharpened his words and defined his face when he talked about his sons' futures. If I didn't think of something fast, my Calloway apprenticeship would be good as gone.

I was no great shakes at arguing a point with Papa, and thanks to my uncle, it might've been easier to empty the Lampasas River with a bucket than change his mind about my taking on more schooling. By the time Uncle Nate left, Papa was convinced that Galveston could provide enough money to see all three of his sons through college, and he was running full chisel to make sure we had that chance. Still, I had to try.

I waited till I caught him sitting alone on the porch

to remind him of how much he'd already taught me about woodworking, and how more than anything I wanted to be a builder, just like he was. He let me talk, but I could see it wasn't doing much good. I finally threw up my hands. "I just ain't got what it takes to be a doctor, Papa."

"*Haven't*, Seth. The correct verb is *haven't*."

I blew out a frustrated breath. My whole life had just gone to blazes, and he was correcting my grammar.

I knew Papa had never had a chance at much formal schooling, but I'd seen him study every book and paper we brought into the house. There wasn't much he didn't know, and little he'd tolerate when it came to incorrect language or bad manners. He'd been known to rap a grown man's knuckles with a knife handle just for reaching across the table for the salt instead of asking for it. Later, Mama told him he'd been lucky the man was good-natured enough to not lay him flat.

I knew early on how much Papa valued education. That was why I'd stuck with school when all my friends had gone on to find paying jobs. I'd promised him I'd graduate before I applied for a carpenter's apprenticeship at Calloway, more for his peace of mind than mine. It was a promise I planned to keep, but I sure didn't want to put my life on hold for longer than that.

"If you don't like medicine," he said, "then we'll look into law, or maybe engineering."

"But, Papa, it's not what I want. You know that."

His jaw tightened, and his leathery face took on a hard, whittled look. "You're too young to know what you want," he said, and the discussion was over.

Far ahead, the engine belched steam and the train slowed. Kate blinked, roused by the scuffle of passengers putting away leftover food, gathering bundles, and straightening hats. She raised her head, and wet curls stuck to her heat-flushed cheek. I pushed her off my lap and onto the seat beside me, but she scrambled right back up again. She leaned across my shoulder, peering out the window for a better look at what was ahead.

"Is that Galveston out there, Seth?"

"Yeah, that's Galveston. Sit down."

"Where's Uncle Nate?"

"Don't worry; he'll be there. Now sit down like I told you."

"But I can't see him. Where is he?"

Matt, always quick to show his impatience, rolled his eyes and let out a groan.

I glared at him, sitting there like he was the biggest toad in the puddle. What did *he* have to complain about? *I* was the one who always had to watch out for Kate. *I* was the one who was expected to answer all her fool questions.

"He's waiting for us at the train station," I said, which seemed to satisfy her for the moment.

She slid onto the seat, but it wasn't long before she was tugging at my damp sleeve. "Seth?" she asked in that baby voice of hers. "Can I sit with Mama?"

I gladly shooed her across the aisle, where she squeezed past Papa and climbed onto Mama's lap.

We left the bay and trestle behind, along with the breezy heat that pumped through the windows, and pulled into Union Passenger Station. The air inside the car turned sluggish and stifling, driving everyone toward the doors like cattle to water troughs, but there was little relief. The close, noisy throng mingled around the station platform, blocking the breeze that swept in from the Gulf of Mexico, making it all but impossible to find Uncle Nate.

I caught the scent of fresh-cut wood and turned to get a quick look down the harbor. Lumber, grain, and mountains of canvas-covered cotton bales sat waiting to be loaded onto great coal-burning ships headed to foreign ports. Farther down the wharf, I saw crates with black lettering—tea, beet sugar—and big bundles of sisal for rope. Dark men, shining with sweat, worked at hauling them into the long tin-roofed sheds lining the docks.

Matt climbed onto a bench, searching across a sea of bowlers, straw hats, and bonnets piled high with ribbons and feathers. "I think I see him, Papa," he said, pointing toward the street. "He brought a buggy. Looks like he brought a dray, too, for the trunks."

Mama slipped up beside me and pushed Kate's hand into mine. I groaned but felt an immediate sense of guilt. Mama looked pale and wilted in her heavy gray traveling suit. Papa had tried to get her to wear something cooler, but she'd refused.

"First impressions are important, Thomas," she'd argued, pointing her finger at him. "And you should wear your Sunday best, as well."

While Papa waited for Mama to pass Kate on to me, he ran a finger around his tight collar, clearly uncomfortable in his only suit. Served him right, I thought. He sure didn't mind sentencing *me* to a life of starched collars.

"Take her for me, Seth," Mama said, "just till I can catch my breath."

She applied an embroidered handkerchief to the sweat bubbling on her forehead and upper lip, patted my shoulder with a gloved hand, and headed toward the carriage with Papa. Matt and Lucas ran after them, leaving me to pull Kate through the noisy crowd alone.

By the time I got to the street, Mama and Papa had finished their greetings and Uncle Nate was instructing his hired man, Ezra, to help them into the carriage. When they were seated, the old man lifted Kate and set her down beside Mama with a "There you be, little missy."

She stared into his watery eyes with that wide-eyed look all kids seem to have for anyone different. It made me realize how few colored men she'd seen in her short four years, and none of them had ever been close enough to lift her into a buggy.

Ezra walked a few steps behind us to finish loading our trunks on the flatbed dray, and Kate said, "Papa, that man is black as ashes. Did he get burned?"

Papa laughed. "Dogs and horses come in different colors, don't they, little Kate?"

"But he's not a horse, is he, Papa?"

"No, he's not a horse." He patted her on the head. "But colored folk aren't much different."

I stared at him. I hadn't been around many coloreds, either, but I'd never heard Papa say anything unkind about them. Others, maybe, but not Papa. I watched him smile at Kate and felt his words sour inside me. I tossed a quick glance at Ezra. He'd surely heard, but the man never blinked an eye.

I squeezed into the carriage next to Matt, and Uncle Nate called out to Archer, urging the horse south down Rosenberg, right into the gulf breeze. The scent of sweaty animals gave way to sweet salt air, and the clop of hooves on the wooden paving blocks set up a rhythm that made me feel like I was still on the train.

We crossed Strand Avenue. "The greatest banking and finance center between New Orleans and San Francisco," Uncle Nate boasted. Then we passed Ship's Mechanic Row, Market, Post Office, and Church streets. I quickly found myself in the midst of the largest architectural display I'd ever seen. For a brief time, I forgot all about college and my cursed fate. While my uncle pointed out markets and dry-goods stores, churches and opera houses, I was taking in the ornate cast-iron storefronts.

I saw tapestries of raised and recessed bricks, and stucco surfaces that sculpted the island's strong sun into light-and-shadow effects I'd never seen the likes of before. Then I noticed that all the buildings had slate roofs and asked Uncle Nate why.

"Because of the Great Conflagration of 1885," he said. "That fire left forty blocks of the city in ashes and destroyed more than four hundred homes. After that, Galveston outlawed wood shingles. Slate has worked pretty well so far."

Ahead of us, in the middle of Rosenberg and Broadway, stood the new Texas Heroes Monument that had been erected just four months ago. The tall bronze statue of Victory pointed toward the bay and beyond, to the San Jacinto battlegrounds on the mainland. "A reminder," Uncle Nate said, "of all the men who fought and died in the Texas Revolution."

We turned west at the monument, down an esplanade

of palms and oleanders, live oak and Mexican dagger. Broadway was considered the spine of the island, the highest point between the gulf on the south and the bay on the north, and all of it appeared to be a showplace for the wealthy. Palacelike homes draped in vines sat as much as three stories high atop raised basements. Behind trimmed jungles of fig, orange, and magnolia trees, I saw bay windows and cupolas, scrolled and spindled trim, wraparound porches and decorative iron gates, and all of it beat inside me like my own heart.

I could tell Papa felt it, too. He sat up straight, eyes wide, taking in every detail, too excited to keep still. His jaw twitched, his knee bounced, his fingers drummed against his leg, and it was right then I knew.

I couldn't give up on what I wanted any more than he could.

Chapter

2

We turned south onto Thirty-fifth Street, and our wheels crunched along a sun-dazzled oyster-shell road. A breeze swept in from the gulf, and I had to grab my hat to keep it from blowing away. Uncle Nate reined Archer in front of a two-story Victorian, and Ezra pulled Deuce and the dray up beside the raised brick basement.

"You can rest here tonight," Uncle Nate said, "and tackle the unpacking at the rental in the morning."

I jumped down, already taking in the house, the large veranda draped in vines, and the barn out back. With the dray, the buggy, and the hired man, it appeared Uncle Nate had done well for himself here in Galveston. This was far grander than what we'd had in Lampasas, and when I looked at Mama, her eyes shimmered with excitement.

Aunt Julia waved at us from the top step while ten-month-old Elliott squirmed in her arms. His older brothers, Andy and Will, dropped to the ground from a tall ash tree in the front yard and headed straight for the buggy.

The four boys were stair-stepped in age—Matt and Lucas, twelve and ten; Andy and Will, eleven and nine. From behind, they looked pretty much the same, like cookies cut from the same dough, but face-on it was another story. We'd all inherited the Braeden dark hair, but Andy and Will had gotten a double dose of Aunt Julia's freckles, making my two younger cousins look a bit like speckled hens. I grinned at the thought. I didn't know the boys all that well, but if they were anything at all like Matt and Lucas, they wouldn't cotton well to hearing themselves compared to chickens.

After a round of quick hellos, there arose such a ruckus from the four boys I couldn't tell who was saying what, but I guess Matt and Lucas understood enough. They ran off to the rope ladder dangling from a large limb and scrambled up to Andy and Will's tree fort. I was relieved to see them go. I'd had enough kicking, elbowing, and cutting shines for one day. In fact, I didn't care if they wanted to stay up there till school started.

"I wanna play, too, Mama," Kate whined, pointing to the tree.

Laughing, Papa jumped from the carriage and swung her to the ground. "You don't want to play with a bunch of wild boys, do you, little Kate?"

She gave him a wide-eyed solemn nod, and Papa just grinned and shook his head.

"Where's Ben?" I asked.

"Delivering groceries for Unger's," Uncle Nate said, "trying to make some money before college starts."

"Dang," I whispered, then glanced quick at Mama to make sure I hadn't been heard. You couldn't utter a word around her that even sounded like swearing, not if you wanted to keep your ears attached to your head. "So he's decided to go to medical school?" I asked.

Uncle Nate nodded. "Real soon."

I caught myself wondering if medicine was what Ben really wanted or if he'd been railroaded into it like me. I didn't wonder long, though. Ben always did have a light about him, something clean and simple that no amount of bad seemed to touch. If anyone should be a doctor, it was him.

And now that I was thinking on it, Lucas just might have a smattering of that, too. I'd seen him pluck ants and june bugs from his bathwater because he couldn't stand to see them drown. And this spring, he'd nursed a newborn orphaned mouse he'd found in the brush behind the house. Mama complained that the last thing this world needed was another mouse, but he wouldn't give it up till it was big enough to eat on its own.

"Come on up and rest in the shade," Aunt Julia

called down to us. "I've made lemonade. You must be exhausted after that hot trip."

We left the boys in their tree fort, climbed the steps, and collapsed into wicker chairs lining the shady veranda. A salty breeze ruffled the red geraniums flanking the door and loosened wisps of hair from Mama's pins. She looked relieved, though the air felt almost too warm for breathing.

"It's been such a hot August," Aunt Julia told us, turning her face to the wind. "And oh, what rain! Overflows were two feet deep in the streets."

"Aw, you know the kids loved it, Julia," Uncle Nate said. "They put on their bathing suits and paddled around in washtubs for hours."

"Even so, I'm thankful the month is almost over. Maybe September will bring us a blue norther."

"Then we'll have to listen to everyone moan because it's too cold to go swimming."

Aunt Julia made a face at him, and Mama laughed. "But Nate says this weather is the best ever for surf bathing and that the gulf is brimming-full and warm as bathwater."

Aunt Julia nodded. "That it is, Eliza, and you and Thomas can see for yourselves soon."

"After supper, if you're up for it," Uncle Nate said.

I was more than ready, but it wouldn't be near as much fun if Ben didn't get home in time to go with us.

Ben was a little older than me, but we'd always gotten on well. In his letters, he'd mentioned catching redfish and trout in the shallows of Galveston Bay and at a place called East End Flats. It was the one thing I'd been looking forward to—that and swimming in the gulf. Public schools wouldn't open here till October, and I had every intention of making the most of my free time.

While Mama and Kate played with Elliott, Aunt Julia fetched her pitcher of cold lemonade from the icebox and passed glasses all around. I took mine to the end of the veranda before I could get stuck with Kate again and leaned against the railing.

Seagulls, wings outstretched, rode the wind just yards in front of me, and farther out, spoonbills shot across the sky like pink arrows. They appeared to be headed west, to a marshy blue glimmer Uncle Nate had called Woollam's Lake, not far from the new Denver Resurvey where we'd be renting.

After a while Mama and Aunt Julia went in to start supper, and behind me, I heard my uncle's voice rise in pitch, reminding me of the day he'd talked Papa into moving. He mentioned the new construction job on Sealy Avenue that Papa would be in charge of. "A grand house," he said, "with rounded bays and porches." I half-listened, more occupied with kids, dogs, and passing carriages than with hearing how Papa would soon be doing everything he was denying me.

I saw a flash of blue and turned my attention to a buggy down the street near Broadway. A girl had stepped out with an armload of packages, and I leaned over the spindled railing for a better look. She shifted her parcels, offered an awkward wave to a friend inside the buggy, and turned toward a front-gabled cottage. I watched her run up the steps, her straw-blond hair swishing from side to side, her shiny blue dress lit with the sun, and as she disappeared inside, I heard Papa mention my name.

"Seth's a good worker. He could handle the job, I'm sure."

Uncle Nate nodded. "Might as well let the boy save toward his own college tuition, right?"

I stared at them, a wrathy heat already building inside me. They were planning my life again, probably lining up delivery work like Ben was doing just so I could help pay for those blasted college classes I never wanted in the first place. I thought about all the fishing days this would cost me, and my anger swelled.

Well, it wouldn't do them any good. I might work the job, but I'd made up my mind about a few things. I'd be planning my own future from now on, and college wasn't figured into any part of it.

Uncle Nate turned in his seat. "Seth, I think we've got some news you might be interested in."

I glanced at Papa, but as usual, his eyes didn't tell me a thing.

"A man named George Farrell," Uncle Nate said, "is foreman for a half block of rentals going up east of here, near the beach. He told me yesterday that he'd lost two men, and I told him that I thought you could easily fill one of those positions."

Shock must've shown all over me, because he took one look at my face and laughed out loud. He patted an arm on the wicker chair beside him and said, "Sit down, boy. I can't tell whether you're mad or glad."

But I couldn't move. I looked at Papa, full of questions, and he nodded.

"It's a real offer, Seth. You can work as a carpenter's helper until school starts, as long as you agree to save three-quarters of your pay toward college."

I opened my mouth, shut it again, then managed a "Yessir, I'll save it."

"Good," Uncle Nate said. "Then you can start Tuesday after Labor Day. You should be settled into the new place by then." He pulled a piece of paper from his pocket. "Here's the address. You'll work every day but Sunday. Think you can handle that?"

"Yessir, I can. Thank you, Uncle Nate."

Smiling, he turned back to Papa, and while they discussed the latest building trends, I just stood there, too amazed at my good fortune to hear a word they were saying.

For weeks I'd been stewing in my own misery, and now, in just four days, I'd be working as a real carpenter. This was my chance to prove to Papa that I had talent, to make him realize that I needed to work with my hands—outside where I could breathe. And if I had to put money aside for classes I'd never attend, so be it.

I turned my face to the salty wind, toward the beach where I'd be working.

Come Tuesday, I'd show him.

Chapter

3

Papa and Uncle Nate disappeared into the study, and I sat outside to watch for Ben. I finally saw him walking down Avenue L, his hair dripping with sweat, his face blotchy red from the heat.

I surprised him as he came around the corner, and he let out a whoop. "Seth!" he bellowed, shaking my hand and slapping me on the shoulder. "Glad you finally made it."

I shrugged and grinned back at him. "Yeah, me too. Things are looking up. Uncle Nate found me a job."

He pulled a handkerchief from his back pocket and wiped his sweaty face. "Not as a delivery boy, I hope. Today I hauled two hundred dollars' worth of groceries in this heat. Can you believe it? Two hundred!"

I let out a low whistle. "Then I guess you'll be too tired to go to the beach later, huh?"

He laughed. "The beach is what we live for around here."

We finished an early supper of fried chicken, okra, and cantaloupe, but we couldn't leave till all the chores were done. The younger boys got stuck washing dishes, and for once, I found myself sitting outside with the grown-ups. I shot Matt a wide grin, and he stuck out his tongue.

As the sun slid toward the west, I noticed more and more people promenading along the streets. Some strolled as if they had no destination in mind, but most poured south toward the beach, with an eager, almost impatient gait. I leaned against the rail with Ben, watching the parade, and the girl I'd seen earlier came bouncing down her steps. She wore a wide-brimmed straw hat and carried a small bundle.

I nudged Ben. "Who's that?"

He called to her, and she waved. "Ella Rose Covington," he said. "Sixteen. Her mother died last year, and now she lives alone with her father. Goes to Ursuline Academy." He tossed me a sly grin. "Too bad she won't be going to public school like you."

"Yeah," I muttered. "Too bad."

Andy and Will burst through the screen door, followed by Matt and Lucas. "We're finished, Ma," Will said. "Can we go?"

The four boys waited, eyes fixed on Aunt Julia's face, bare feet twitching, but she pretended not to notice.

"Ma-a-a," Andy whined. His freckled face puckered in exasperation.

Aunt Julia laughed. "You can go ahead of us if you agree to stay within the first ropes. *But,*" she said, holding up a finger, "if I find out any of you disobeyed, there'll be no more swimming until school starts. Have I made myself clear?"

"Yes, ma'am!"

Andy and Will raced for the steps. Lucas tossed a quick thank-you over his shoulder and scrambled after them. Matt, however, leaned down and gave Aunt Julia a kiss on the cheek. "I'll make sure they stay inside the ropes," he whispered.

She watched him go, then turned to Mama. "That Matt is one sweet boy, Eliza. You must be very proud of him."

It nearly made me puke. Matt was born knowing which side of his bread to butter, and he did it well.

Ben and I left our lagging parents behind to follow as best they could and headed east down Avenue N. I was glad to get away. I never knew when Mama might shove Kate at me again.

We passed the Garten Verein with its croquet greens and tennis courts, its clubhouse and bowling alleys, and the bright, octagon-shaped dancing pavilion tiered like a massive wedding cake. In the next block, Ben pointed out the Ursuline convent, and beyond that,

Ursuline Academy, where the blond-headed girl down the street would go. Her classes would start next week.

"But that's a whole month earlier than public schools," I said. "I bet she's not happy about that."

"What? You mean you're not looking forward to school?"

"Are you kidding?"

Ben grinned and shrugged. "Right now, I can't think of much else."

I shook my head in disbelief. "You're really going to be a doctor, huh? Live a life filled with blood and guts?"

He tossed me a surprised look. "Papa told me you were planning to go into medicine yourself. Did he get it wrong?"

"Yeah, he did—for sure. My *father* is the one planning that career. I'm going to be a carpenter."

Ben raised an eyebrow and gave a slow nod. "You're in a fix, then, aren't you? According to Papa, Uncle Thomas has a powerful stubborn streak. Sounds like you'll need all the luck you can get to squirm out of this one."

I laughed, but he was dead right.

We turned south on Twenty-fourth Street and joined a stream of families walking to the great bathhouses built on pilings out over the water. The Pagoda Company's twin buildings lay just ahead. Their sloping roofs of striped canvas made them look more like two giant circus tents staked out in the gulf than a bathhouse. As we neared the beach, I saw Murdoch's, too, and beyond that, the three-story Olympia.

Voices rose and fell on the wind, and I turned east toward what must've been ten blocks of ramshackle buildings.

"That's the Midway," Ben said, pulling me in for a closer look.

The air sizzled with frying clams and frankfurters, and rang with shouts from swimmers and cries from excited gulls. Merchants hawked seashells and salt-water taffy, kewpie dolls and satin pillows, and bellowed invitations to "step right up." We walked past swimmers with beach balls tucked under their arms lined up next to people in street clothes, waiting for a chance at the penny arcades. And farther down the beach, I spotted a trestle that stretched out over the surf and back again.

"Trolleys go out over the water?"

"Sure. Some people want to experience the gulf high and dry." He grinned. "Not everyone's as brave as we are."

The way the beach looked today, I couldn't imagine there'd be anyone left in town to take the trolley. It seemed most all of Galveston was here this evening, bathing, bicycling, or just driving carriages across the crisp-smooth sand.

We chose the Pagoda for changing into our suits and

took their long boardwalk that started at the end of Twenty-fourth Street. The steps took us high above the beach, and, once out over the surf, I stopped to look down at the crowds gathered around ropes and barnacled pilings. They jumped waves in dark wool bathing suits, looking more like fleas on a stray dog's ear than swimmers.

All except one.

I leaned out over the weathered handrail spotted white from gulls and tried to get a better look. My stomach fluttered, then lurched hard. It was the girl with sun-bright hair. At least it looked like her. By the time I glanced up again, Ben was gone, and I had to hurry to catch up.

When we'd changed and finally gotten back to the beach, I saw Mama and waved. She looked a bit unsure of herself as she waved back at me from the door of a brightly painted portable bathhouse. A parade of these two-wheeled wagons lined the beach, waiting to be rolled out into the water a short way and hauled back in by horses, a convenience for swimmers who wanted to keep sand out of their stockings and shoes. I had to laugh, thinking of Mama inside, gripping the walls while the concessionaire pushed her toward the surf.

While Ben and I bobbed in the water and rode the waves, I watched for the yellow-haired girl. I kept an eye on the warm surf around the Pagoda and under the splashy lettering painted across the side of the building where I'd last seen her. *A Ride on the Katy Is Like a Drive on the Beach,* the sign for MK & T Railway declared. I must've read those words a hundred times before the sky settled into layers of pink and purple and I had to accept that I'd missed her. I hauled my heavy limbs from the surf, feeling like a dunce for letting her tangle up my thoughts the way she had. I didn't even know her and probably never would.

Ben and I changed back into our street clothes while sunset colors slid away. By the time we started home, there was nothing left but twinkling silver in a black umbrella sky. The electric lamps, perched high on tall pilings out in the surf, flickered on, and I heard cheers from late-night swimmers.

"Skinny-dippers," Ben said, grinning. "They swim just beyond the light—sometimes as many as two hundred men—naked as the day they were born."

I shook my head and laughed. It was hard to imagine.

We took Twenty-fourth Street back to Avenue N where nightfall had transformed the Garten Verein into something out of one of Kate's fairy tales. Electric light spilled across the grounds, gilding leaves and blossoms and ladies' white lace gowns. The open dancing pavilion sparkled through the trees like a great Chinese lantern.

I stopped to listen to the band, to the way the music mingled with the sounds of surf and the soft crash of bowling pins, and I might've stayed far longer if Ben hadn't pulled me away. But it was late, and tomorrow I'd be only three days away from my future.

Chapter 4

Ezra's rooster woke me the next morning, pulling me from something soft and murmuring, dragging me back to my crowded island of mosquito netting. I pushed Matt off my arm, threw back the netting, and stumbled for the door.

Once in the hall, I ran into Mama, holding a step stool and pulling Kate behind her. She gave me a sleepy look and held a finger to her lips. "Where are you going?" she whispered.

"Out back," I said, fully aware of what was coming next.

"Good." She pushed the step stool at me. "Then you can take your sister for me. I've got to get dressed and help with breakfast."

"Mom, I can't. *I* have to go."

"Well, Seth, you're going anyway."

I stared at her for a moment, all rumpled in her tired blue robe. I was tempted to walk down the stairs and leave her standing there, and one day I might. But not today.

Outside, a fiery glow barely flickered on the horizon, and already the sticky-damp heat clung to my skin and sat heavy in my chest. We walked to the backyard, past the small magnolia tree near the side stairs, and swung the outhouse door open. Spiders and cockroaches scrambled for safety while Kate hid her face in my nightshirt.

"Are they gone, yet?" she whispered.

I clenched my teeth, hearing Mama's voice plain as day in my head, saying, "She thinks you're the only one who can get the bugs to go home to their babies."

"Yeah, they're gone." I dropped the stool and kicked it close to the seat. "You can go in now."

"Thank you, Seth," she said, stepping onto the stool.

I closed the door and waited.

"I'm through," she called after a few moments.

I let her out, shooed her toward the house, and pushed the stool aside. "Dang-it-all," I whispered to the walls. "How long can a man be expected to take his baby sister to the toilet?" I stepped back out, and the door slammed shut behind me. I cringed at the sound, but it quickly disappeared on the salt-damp breeze to disturb the neighbors up the street.

Before I headed back, a movement around the small frame house near the alley caught my eye. Ezra was in his garden, cutting okra from tall stalks. A dented pan lay at his feet, already half full of the prickly harvest.

I'd heard Uncle Nate say that he let the colored man live rent-free in the two-room house in exchange for help with horses and chores. He appeared quite handy with a hammer and saw, too. The clapboard siding was bare of paint, but the windows were neatly shuttered and the gables embellished with spindled woodwork, all of which looked in good repair. So were the fences around the garden and chicken pen. While I stood there wondering if he had a wife inside waiting to cook his breakfast, his hands dropped to his sides as if he knew he was being watched. He picked up the pan at his feet, slowly turned, and looked my way.

I waved, feeling a bit embarrassed about my staring, but even more so about the stool dangling from my hand. Ezra hesitated, but only for a moment, then he gave me a wide grin and waved back.

We finished off a breakfast of ham, eggs, and grits, then packed up the few things we'd needed for the night and loaded them back into the buggy. Ezra had already left in the dray, headed for the rental.

Uncle Nate turned Archer west, down Avenue R, taking us past Woollam's Lake. He said there were only about thirty houses in the Denver Resurvey, so Mama was pleased to find we had so many neighbors close by.

"The Masons live next door to your rental," Uncle Nate said, "and Captain Munn, the Vedders, and the Peek family live behind you toward the beach. Richard Peek is our city engineer."

He'd already told us about Fort Crockett, with its brand-new artillery emplacements, which lay just south of us, close to the shoreline. And about Saint Mary's Orphanage, too, which housed ten sisters and almost a hundred children. The two large dormitories sat about ten blocks farther down the island, in the dunes right next to the beach. I couldn't imagine what it was like to lose both your parents, but I figured that if it had to be so, then living in a place where you could go swimming and fishing every day was where I'd want to be.

We pulled up to a small, two-story house facing north, its back turned to the gulf. Like most of the homes in Galveston, it was built atop a raised basement. It had electric lights and a porch, or "gallery" as they called it here, that ran across the main floor and wrapped around the east side to catch the gulf breezes.

Mama looked excited. The house was nicer than anything we'd had in Lampasas. She and Kate climbed the steps to look it over, and Matt and Lucas ran after them. I grabbed one of the few crates left in the dray to carry up with me, but Uncle Nate put his hand on my shoulder.

"Ezra will do that, son."

I stood there, gripping Mama's china while Papa and Uncle Nate continued their talk. I'd always been expected to help before and didn't see why this time should be any different. Besides, Ezra was old, and he'd already made countless trips up those stairs.

"No need a-worryin'," Ezra said, easing the crate from my hands. "I'll take right good care of it, Mr. Seth."

The old man snuggled the china close to his chest and headed up the stairs, mindful of each step to the main floor. Two more trips and the dray sat empty. Uncle Nate said his good-byes and left Ezra to take Papa into town for groceries.

While they were gone, a woman named Virginia Mason came to welcome us with fresh baked bread and a bundle of jasmine cut from the trellis in her yard. The sweet-smelling blossoms reminded me of the honeysuckle that had grown outside my bedroom window in Lampasas. While I put the vines in water for Mama, I heard Mrs. Mason say that she and her husband lived next door with their three children and a servant. "And if we can be of any service in helping you get settled," she said, "please do not hesitate to call upon us."

The fact that so many here had colored servants seemed a curious thing to me. In Lampasas, most had been Mexicans or immigrants who spoke little English.

I never had any firsthand experience with them, though. Mama and Papa had always considered hired help to be an extravagance when they had three strapping boys to help with the heavy work. I grew up scrubbing floors, tending horses, washing clothes—whatever was needed—and it appeared that nothing would change much with this move.

All day Saturday, Mama had us doing things that would've made any man my age balk, dangling the chance to see the Labor Day parade in front of us like it was Christmas morning. While we helped clean the outhouse and unpack dishes, put away our clothes and make our beds, Matt and Lucas talked of nothing but Monday's festivities. But it was Tuesday that pulled hard at *my* thoughts, the day I'd finally get to do the kind of work a man could be proud of.

Over the next few days, more neighbors came with friendly welcomes. There were Mrs. Peek and Mrs. Vedder, who lived behind us on Avenue S; Mrs. Munn from Avenue S ½; and from still nearer the beach, Captain Lucian Minor, who seemed a tad lonely, with his whole family in Virginia for the summer. The Collums, a middle-aged couple with a house full of pets, came, too, talking a steady stream about their cats and parrots, which seemed an unlikely combination to me.

I'd already seen the three young Masons from next

door and most of the six Peek children playing ball in the streets. I'd seen two of the Vedder kids, too, crawling all over their daddy's retired hearse and a gray donkey they called Whiskers. But most of the time it was impossible to pick out who belonged where. There seemed to be plenty of room here for kids, chickens, livestock, and truck gardens, most of which everyone had in abundance. And according to Mrs. Florence Vedder, there was even a bathhouse just six blocks away on the beach.

"We have lots of bathing parties and watermelon feasts for the children there," she told Mama. "We have poker games for the parents, too. Or hugo and whist. And sometimes we do a little moonlight dancing and have refreshments on the bathhouse roof garden." She pointed to the houses around us. "All these families are friends, and we've had many good times together. I'm sure you'll like it here, Eliza."

Mama's smile was even wider that evening when she told Papa about Mrs. Vedder's visit. She sat at the table, teaching Kate how to make paper flowers, and all the while she chattered on and on about what she'd learned.

She seemed to be settling in fast here and not at all upset that she had to start over in a new place. For me it was somewhat different. I didn't miss my friends all that much—they'd quit school long ago to work—but

I was finding it odd eating my meals at a rented table and seeing strange children and strange animals playing up and down the block. Even more peculiar was lying in a bed that wasn't my own, listening to the creaks and sighs of an unfamiliar house at night.

All three of us boys slept in one room with a chiffonier for our clothes and three narrow bunks. I didn't mind the small beds as long as I didn't have to share one with Matt or Lucas, but the bedsprings squeaked differently when I rolled over. And unlike my old bedroom, the curtains were plagued by salt-damp breezes and rarely fell silent. During the first night, I lingered at the open windows while the boys slept, listening to the faint crash of surf against the not-so-distant beach, filling my head with the enormity and sheer power of what lay just out of sight. It made me feel like an ant in a house of sand, with the overfull bowl of the sea lapping at my door.

True to her word, Mama packed a lunch Monday morning, and we met Uncle Nate and his family in town to picnic in the park and watch the afternoon parade. Matt, who was never without his baseball and bat, started a game and quickly pulled in enough players for two teams. When it came time to quit, we almost had to drag him from the park.

The parade turned out to be a splendid sight, with

band music and big floats of every kind. We saw decorated buggies and bicycles, and even dogs and pigs decked out with ribbons as though they were going to the fair.

When it was over, Peightal and Booth, contracting tinners, received first prize for their float, which was in the shape of a star with a huge eagle perched on top— all in tinwork. I heard a reporter from the *Daily News* say, "There seemed to be more good humor, snap, and ginger in this parade than any turnout for the past several years."

We said good-bye to Uncle Nate, Aunt Julia, and the kids, and headed home. Papa bought saltwater taffy for us to eat on the long walk and teased Mama about having been so leery of making this move.

She laughed, her eyes still shiny from the excitement of the parade. "The Good Lord has a reason for everything, Thomas, and I suppose there's a reason for this move as well."

I'd heard Mama say that sort of thing many times before, but I wasn't sure I believed it. Papa didn't reply, but I could tell he thought he already knew why he was here. He wanted to build a new business for himself and send his sons to college. I watched him peel the paper from another piece of taffy and pop it into Mama's mouth—I think just to hear her laugh again.

I liked seeing them happy, but I liked even better

that I'd have a chance to prove myself to Papa. If God truly had a reason for everything that happened to us, then making Papa see things my way had to be the reason I got that carpenter job.

That night, I wound the clock and set the alarm for six. The walk to my new job site in the morning would be a long one, and I had no intention of being late for my first day of work.

But sleep didn't come easy. I lay wide awake for hours, staring at the ceiling while parade cheers and band music played in my head. After a while, I caught the sweet scent of jasmine drifting through the windows from the Masons' trellis next door. It made this strange place feel a bit more like home, and finally I closed my eyes.

Chapter

5

A loud clap of thunder woke me before daylight Tuesday morning. Bedsprings squeaked as Matt and Lucas rolled over and settled into sleep again. I lay there, waiting, and when lightning lit the room, I glanced at the clock. It was almost five.

Thunder rolled again, already sounding farther away. I turned off the alarm and went to the windows. The storm had swept in from the southeast, and as I watched, another blue-white lightning strike turned rooftops and trees into a landscape of winter white and shadow. I groaned. Rain would ruin everything.

But apparently I'd slept through the worst of it. By five thirty, the storm had blown over, and my first day of work lay ahead of me, damp but promising.

I slipped downstairs, ate a cold breakfast of bread and leftover ham, and packed more of the same for later. Careful not to wake anyone, I carried my hat and shoes to the front steps and was down the street before the sun had peeked above the horizon.

The thunderstorm had lowered the temperature slightly, making my walk the most pleasant since I'd arrived. The birds must've felt it, too. Doves cooed and roosters crowed. Seagulls glided overhead till their beady eyes spotted some discarded scrap. Then dozens would appear from nowhere, thieving from one another and starting a fracas of calls.

Block after block, I heard babies wake and cry for their mothers. Doors squeaked open, pans rattled on stoves, and streams of milk from full cows hit empty buckets. I smelled horses and hay, bacon and biscuits, and, before long, a salty breeze lifted the sweet scent of fresh lumber and carried it right to me.

Just ahead, only two blocks from the beach, lay the houses where I'd be working.

I was the first to arrive, and in the long shadows of early morning, I walked through the unfinished houses, each one at a different stage of completion. They'd all been built from one plan but cleverly changed in some way. A side gable here or a front gable there, a different window or door. Arched porch lintels with cutout railings on one, turned posts with Victorian balustrades on another.

I climbed a ladder left leaning against the third house,

stood on the unfinished gallery, and looked out over the gulf. The sun, still low, shimmered across the waves, a reminder of heat yet to come. Even with the slightly cooler breeze, I felt sweat beading under my shirt and trickling down my back. My first day at work would be a hot one.

"Hey!" a voice called from below.

I stepped closer to the unprotected edge of the gallery and glanced below at a young man who looked to be a few years older than me.

"You shouldn't be up there," he said.

"Sorry!" I yelled down, wishing I'd waited on the ground instead of prowling around. "It's my first day, and I guess I was a bit curious."

I climbed down while he watched, his blond hair and blue eyes vivid against a sun-browned face.

"You're the new helper?"

I nodded and held out my hand. "I'm Seth Braeden."

He peered at me from under the brim of his straw hat. "Henry Covington," he said, ignoring my hand. "You look young."

I let my hand fall to my side. "I'm almost seventeen."

"Yeah, like I said. Young. Got any experience?"

"Some."

He gave me a skeptical look, which along with the ignored handshake I took as bad signs. I hadn't been here five minutes and already someone didn't like me. While I stared at him, trying to remember where I'd heard his name, another man arrived.

"You two meet?"

Henry turned, and to my surprise, his attitude toward me seemed to turn just as quickly. "Yessir, Mr. Farrell, we have. This is Seth Braeden, your new man, and he looks pretty able if you ask me."

Mr. Farrell's grin crinkled the corners of his eyes and showed a gap between his front teeth. "Glad to meet you, Seth. Your uncle tells me you're a fine carpenter, almost as good as your father."

"Thank you, Mr. Farrell. I appreciate this opportunity, and I'll sure do my best for you."

He nodded. "Fair enough." He looked past Henry and called out to a young colored man standing barefoot by the raised basement. "Come on over here, boy."

The man trudged through the sand, his dark limbs willow-limber and just as graceful.

"That's Josiah," Mr. Farrell told me. "Now, I allow I wasn't too excited about working a colored boy, but he appears to be a dang good carpenter and minds what he's told. If he gives you trouble, Seth, let me know."

"Yessir," I said, though I couldn't imagine what kind of trouble Mr. Farrell might expect. A closer look at Josiah told me he was younger than I first thought, nearer to my age than Henry's. It was his height that'd fooled me. He looked to be at least six-foot. I nodded my greeting, and he nodded back, barely meeting my eyes before he dropped his gaze back to the ground.

"Let's go to work, boys," Mr. Farrell said.

"But where's Zach? And Frank and Charlie?" Henry asked. "Are we gonna have to work double time to make up for the Three Musketeers today?"

I saw Mr. Farrell's jaw tighten. "I gave the Judson boys time off for the funeral, remember?"

"No, sir; I mean, yessir." Henry's face flushed red. "I guess I did forget about their daddy dying and all."

Mr. Farrell shook his head and turned his back on Henry. "We're working three men short today," he said to me and pointed to the third house. "Think you can build a staircase?"

"Yessir."

"Good. Then you and Henry start on that while me and Josiah finish framing up the top floor. If there's something you're not sure about, ask *before* you cut lumber, not after."

"Yessir," I said again and followed Henry to the third house.

"You weren't trying to hornswoggle the boss, were you?" he asked over his shoulder.

"Hornswoggle?"

"Yeah, about knowing how to build a staircase."

I shook my head. "It's a bit foolish to say you can do something when you can't."

"So how many you built before this one?"

"I've helped my father with a dozen or so, and I've built one by myself."

"One?" He laughed. "Well, I guess that makes you the helper, doesn't it?" He pointed to the lumber in the basement. "You bring out the sawhorses and two-by-twelves, and I'll get the tools."

I ducked my head and trudged off to the basement, wondering how I could prove anything at all to Papa if I had to work with someone like Henry.

Chapter

6

Once Henry stopped talking and started working, I could see why Mr. Farrell put up with his thoughtless remarks. He was a good carpenter. We finished the outside stairs and the balustrade that ran up and around the gallery, then Mr. Farrell put us to trimming windows. When the sun finally sank behind the trees, we packed up our tools and started for home.

Henry lived to the east on Avenue Q, not far from Mr. Farrell, so the two left together. Josiah struck out for the beach, and rather than take my morning route alone, I decided to walk with him. His long strides had taken him three full blocks before I caught up with him. "Hope you don't mind the company," I said, breathing hard.

"No, sir, don't mind." He gave me a quick glance, dropped a half pace behind, then turned his attention back to the ground he was covering.

"Are you going far?"

"No, sir, not far."

He didn't seem too fond of talking, but I'd admired his work more than once today and told him so. He'd anticipated Mr. Farrell's every move, made quick work of figuring and marking his cuts, and I'd never seen anyone saw through boards the way he had.

He listened, then tossed me a look I couldn't quite decipher, something kin to puzzlement, or perhaps surprise. It left me thinking that maybe no one had ever told him just how good a carpenter he was. After several more failed attempts at talking, we walked in silence.

Just before we reached Thirty-fifth Street, where Uncle Nate lived, Josiah nodded his good-bye and turned down the alley. I slowed, trying to keep my eye on where he was going, but he disappeared quick, leaving me to wonder just how close he lived to Uncle Nate.

As I passed Thirty-fifth, I looked long and hard down the street, hoping to catch a glimpse of Ella Rose, the girl with sunshine hair. But I still had a good walk ahead of me, so I didn't dally.

When I got home, I saw Matt, Lucas, and Kate at the Masons' house next door, eating melon with Kearny, Jr., and Francesca.

"Hey!" Matt spit seeds. "Did they sack you yet?"

"Aw, they ain't gonna kick Seth off that job, Matt."
Lucas grinned at me. "He's almost good as Papa."

Kate dropped her rind and jumped into my arms.
"Where you been, Seth?" she asked, her breath sweet
from the melon. "I waited and waited."

I pulled her sticky fingers from my neck and let her
slide back to the ground. "Come on, Kate," I said,
ignoring the boys. "You need cleaning up."

We both washed up out back, and after sending Kate
in to Mama, I took the back stairs to the kitchen. Supper was long over, but Mama had left me a plate in the
oven. I poured myself a glass of milk, and while I
wolfed down my meal, Papa came in with a newspaper
tucked under his arm and a cup in his hand.

"How'd it go?" he asked, reaching for the coffeepot
at the back of the stove.

I swallowed a mouthful of potato. "Good, Papa, very
good. And you?"

He swished the pot, gauging its contents. "The
same." He managed to fill his cup half full, gave me a
slight smile, and headed back to the parlor to read his
paper.

Like always, I wondered what was behind his smile.
Was he proud that I'd done a man's work today, or just
glad that I was saving toward college?

It was different with Mr. Farrell. "Good work, Seth,"

he'd said, and that wide, gapped grin of his told me that he meant it. I couldn't remember ever hearing Papa say words like that. Not to me. Not to any of us.

An unexpected bitterness welled in my throat. I swallowed hard, jerked up my dirty dishes, and slid them into the sink.

After washing up, I stepped outside, onto the east gallery. In the distance I heard the lulling sound of surf rolling onto the beach. With the sky so clear, surely there wouldn't be any thunderstorms tonight. I stretched, already feeling the achy tightness that twelve hours' labor brings when you're not used to it. Tomorrow I'd work that soreness out, but I didn't see how I could work away the bitterness inside me if Papa kept adding to it every day.

The three Judson brothers arrived early Wednesday wearing black mourning bands around their shirtsleeves. One glance and I knew Frank and Charlie were twins—same nose, same crooked teeth, same cowlick in their identical brown hair. They looked to be about twenty, some years younger than their brother.

Zachary Judson already had the markings of a working carpenter—that leathery brown skin with the tiny hatch lines that would eventually deepen, like mud cracking under a scorching sun. I'd seen it happen to Papa and knew that it was in my future as well.

Mr. Farrell introduced me to the Judson boys, and after I'd offered my condolences, he put me and Josiah to work with Zach.

I liked Zach right off, and I think Josiah did, too. The man didn't say much, but when he did, I heard a slow easiness behind his words. I followed on his heels all morning, doing whatever he asked, but always watching. There was something almost mystifying in the way he rested saw and nail against lumber—just for a second—like he was listening, like the wood had whispered something to him I couldn't quite hear.

After our noon meal, I began to notice a connection between the three of us, an invisible rhythm that bound us one to the other. We danced to music only we could hear. One set of hands. A single purpose.

I was startled later to see the sun sinking below the tree line. Like chickens picking off june bugs, we'd finished one job after another, and the hours had disappeared clean and without notice. I looked back, surprised at what we'd accomplished. I think Mr. Farrell was, too.

"Well, I swan," he said, pushing his straw hat back off his forehead, "if you three don't make a dang good team." He walked off with a grin on his face, shaking his head. "Bright and early tomorrow, boys," he hollered over his shoulder. "Bright and early."

I helped put away the lumber and tools, then said

my good-byes. Zach nodded and headed north with his brothers. They'd said very little about themselves, but Henry had already told me about their mama passing last summer. And now their daddy was gone, too, leaving Zach with eight younger brothers and sisters to worry over. Curious about where he lived, I watched him till he turned east on Avenue P, then hurried after Josiah. He'd already lit out for the beach, like yesterday.

This time, I didn't talk much, at least not at first. I didn't have any idea where Josiah's thoughts were, but mine were a jumble of captured moments that played and replayed in my head. And all of them had to do with Zach and the way he worked. But even so, it wasn't long before I remembered that I still didn't know anything about him. Like yesterday, he'd been keeping a half pace behind me, which made talking difficult, so I slowed down and matched my steps with his. Confusion flickered across his face, and I saw a definite hesitation in his gait, but he kept to my pace.

"I was wondering," I said to him. "Do you live with your parents?"

"No, sir. I lives with my granddaddy."

"Just the two of you?"

"Yessir."

"Oh."

He never raised his eyes to look at me.

"Well, I noticed that you turned down the alley

behind my uncle's house yesterday. Maybe you know him? Nathan Braeden?"

He tossed me a quick glance. "Yessir, I knows Mister Braeden. My granddaddy works for 'im."

"Your grandfather is Ezra?"

"Yessir."

I grinned at him. "I stayed at my uncle's house just this past Friday. Ezra helped us get moved into our rental the next morning."

"I knows. Satdy was my first workday or I woulda hepped. It were Mister Braeden that got me my job."

I laughed. "He got me my job, too."

Josiah never looked me in the eye, but he smiled slightly before he turned down the alley.

"See you tomorrow," I called.

"Yessir," he called back.

I shook my head. No one had ever called me sir before, especially not someone my own age, and it just didn't sit right.

I shot a quick glance down Thirty-fifth Street, and when I didn't see Ella Rose, I let my thoughts turn back to work, back to those frozen moments in my head, back to that . . . that thing that had passed from Zach right into me.

I'd felt it wake something inside me, and I think Josiah did, too. A quiet something that'd always been waiting in my hands and suspended in my every word to Papa. Today, it shot right through me, lighting me up like the electrical current that lit the city, bridging each of us to our work and to one another, twilight-soft one minute, then strong enough to light the whole world the next. I didn't understand it, not a bit of it, but thanks to Zach, I recognized it. I'd glimpsed it before—this undercurrent that had been sleeping in me ever since I could remember.

Now if I could only bring it to life, make it shine in me the way it did in Zach. Then Papa would know. He'd see I was a true carpenter, and that I could never be anything else.

Chapter

7

I came home Wednesday evening to find kids all over the yard. Kate sat on the steps with two neighbor girls, Katherine Vedder and Francesca Mason, jars of lightning bugs in their laps. The black bugs snapped and clicked against the glass, and Kate, grinning, held hers up for me to see.

I heard counting coming from behind an umbrella chinaberry tree next door and saw a handful of Peek children scramble for good hiding places before the count reached ten. And out in the street, the boys hadn't given up on their game, even though the day's light was almost gone.

Jacob Vedder tossed a ball into the air and swung his bat. A loud crack sent Matt and Jacob's cousin Allen sliding across the dirt after a fly ball. Clouds of dust billowed into open windows, and when Matt came up victorious, he reared back to throw the ball to Jacob.

But something stopped him.

He stood there, arm flung back, staring at a young colored boy not much bigger than Kate. I'd seen the boy watching at the edge of the road, eyes wide and eager, bare toes digging into the dirt.

"Come on, Matt," Lucas complained. "Throw it."

Matt just stood there, his face a puzzle. He slowly lowered his arm. "What's your name?" he asked the boy.

"Toby."

Matt nodded. "Well, here you go, Toby," he said, tossing the ball to him. "Jacob's waiting."

Toby pitched the ball back and sat down in the dirt again, a grin of pure pleasure on his face. For such a little fella, he had a dang good arm on him, but it was Matt who'd surprised me most. He rarely showed this generous side of himself, not to me anyway. I glanced at Lucas, and saw amazement skitter across his face, too.

I remembered Mama's words about there being a good reason for everything that happens, and shrugged. Maybe a bit of Galveston was what Matt had needed all along.

I squeezed around the girls and took the steps up to the gallery two at a time. Mama and Papa sat outside on the east end, catching the breeze and watching the kids play. They waved at me, and Mama hollered, "Supper's in the oven."

I waved back, already headed for the kitchen.

Thursday morning, I skipped my usual route down Broadway and took Avenue N instead, the same way Ben and I had walked to the beach last Friday. Sunrise colors faded to a cloudless blue sky as I approached the Garten Verein. Unlike my first night here, I heard no band music, no crash of bowling pins, no laughter, but it did make me long for the beach again. As much as I liked my job, I found myself looking forward to Saturday evening after work. Ben and I planned to meet at the Pagoda bathhouse again, and on Sunday, we were going fishing.

I turned south by Ursuline Academy, and my heart nearly skipped right out of my chest. Ella Rose stood in front of me, about ten yards away, hair shining, blue eyes smiling.

"You must be Ben's cousin," she said, walking up to me. "Seth, right? I'm Ella Rose Covington. Henry told me what a good carpenter you are."

I couldn't seem to get my mouth open. "Um . . . Henry?"

"My cousin, Henry Covington. He said you work together?"

"Oh, that's right. We do. It's a pleasure to meet you."

"Thank you." She gave me a bright smile. "You know, I think I saw you when I was swimming last Friday."

I nodded, my thoughts a stubborn knot I couldn't work loose. "I . . . um . . . think I saw you, too. You were in the water?"

"Yes." She laughed. "And you were looking over the Pagoda railing, right?"

My head bobbed again. "I looked for you later, but I guess you were gone by then."

"You did? That was sweet of you."

She shot me another radiant smile, and a fierce flutter racked my belly.

"Will you be going back this weekend?" she asked.

"Yes, Saturday—Saturday after work, for sure." I sucked in a deep breath, trying to still the quiver in my knees. "Will I see you there?"

"Oh, I'm sure you will—me and half of Galveston." She laughed again, then tossed a quick glance at the academy. "Sister Agnes promised to help me with my Latin if I came in early, so I have to hurry." She shifted her books. "See you Saturday," she called over her shoulder.

"Yes, Saturday," I said, waving.

I stood there by the road, staring after her. "Covington," I muttered. "Of course. She's Henry's cousin. Stupid, stupid, stupid!"

A group of passing girls heard me and giggled. Red-faced, I took off for work.

Mr. Farrell put me with Zach and Josiah again. "At the rate you boys are going," he said, "we'll make our deadline and get that bonus yet."

For the first time, I saw a big smile on Zach's face. I guess he really needed the money with so much family to care for. It made me eager to make sure he got it, not that I couldn't find a good use for the extra pay myself. I wondered if Ella Rose went to dances at the pavilion. If I ever hoped to take her, I'd have to look into buying some decent clothes, though after putting away three-quarters of my pay, the rest wouldn't go very far. I remembered the way the Garten Verein had looked Friday night, and I could almost see Ella Rose standing under a leafy canopy in front of the pavilion, brilliant light casting a halo of silver around her like . . .

I felt a nudge, blinked, and Ella Rose disappeared.

"You all right?" Zach asked, his arms full of lumber.

"Yeah, I'm okay." I ducked my head, hoping he wouldn't see the sudden heat I felt in my cheeks. I grabbed the sawhorses and carried them up the stairs.

By afternoon, a few clouds had rolled in and the wind shifted to the north, bringing a hint of prairie and mesquite, hills and home. I breathed it in, but there was something else, too, tingling at the edge of my senses. I stood by the raised basement, letting the feeling grow inside me, and remembered: A north wind always brought change.

Mr. Farrell must've sensed something, too. He stood on the gallery, looking out over the gulf, his face furrowed with an edgy bewilderment. I looked, too, but couldn't figure out what had caught his attention. The tide was high and the water rough, yet despite the peculiar haze in the sky and the fresh northerly wind, the gulf still swelled and rolled onto the beach like it had since the day I'd arrived.

As the day wore on, we all seemed to move slower. The north breeze had done nothing to lessen the heat, as I'd hoped. In fact, it grew even sultrier, sitting heavy on my brow and in my chest, weighing me down till every breath was an effort. I soon forgot about Ella Rose, and by sunset, all I wanted to do was go home and fall asleep by the open windows.

I'd set the clock to go off earlier Friday morning, and when the alarm sounded, I jumped to turn it off. Lucas groaned, and Matt muttered, "Can't you put a pillow over that thing?"

"Go back to sleep," I whispered, jerking on my pants. I carried my best work shirt downstairs with me, washed up outside, and took extra care in combing my hair. There was a good chance I'd run into Ella Rose again this morning.

I headed for the kitchen to pack my noon meal and found Mama wrist-deep in bread dough. There'd be six brown loaves sitting on the stove when I came in this evening. She tilted her big bowl, turned the pale mound onto the floured table, and began the rhythmic push and fold of kneading. Kate, feet still bare, danced back and forth on the wood floor behind her.

"Would you take her to the outhouse before you go, Seth, so I can finish up this bread?"

I groaned. Didn't she know I had a real job, now, like Papa?

"Mama," I said, "I can't keep doing this. I'm not a kid anymore."

She paused slightly in her rhythm, and without ever looking up, said simply, "I know, Seth."

I stared at her, waiting for something more, some glimpse of understanding. When it didn't come, I grabbed Kate's hand, pulled her to the door and down the stairs. By the time I got back in, Mama had finished her kneading and was packing my dinner. She smiled her thanks, but I was too irritated to smile back. Things would never change around here, and I had to face that fact. She and Papa might never see me as a grown man, no matter what I did. Without a word, I grabbed up my dinner and headed for the door.

The still-dark sky looked clear but felt unusually warm and humid when I left. I wasn't two minutes down the road before I was wiping sweat from my face and swatting mosquitoes. The bit of rain left in the gutters from Tuesday night's storm had spawned some mean little devils, and they all seemed to have a rabid appetite for my neck.

The sun was up when I got to Ursuline Academy, but I saw no sign of Ella Rose. I stood waiting, my shirt streaked with sweat and my handkerchief grimy. After a short while, I finally saw her halfway down the block and ran to meet her.

I must've looked a mess by the time I caught up with her. She took one look at my sweaty face, laughed, and pulled a lace-trimmed handkerchief from her sleeve.

I stared at the embroidered initials in the corner, about to refuse her offer, but found myself reaching for it anyway, sliding it across my forehead and my upper lip. It smelled sweet, like lilacs. I started to hand it back to her, then saw what I'd done to her fresh handkerchief. My cheeks flushed hot.

"Keep it," she said, pulling out a second one. "You might need it later." She patted at the moisture beading on her own forehead and neck, then laughed at the sullied cloth. "Where does all this grime come from?"

I shrugged, smiling at the effortless way she'd set me at ease.

She glanced over at the academy and sighed. "I have to go."

"See you tomorrow?" I asked.

She nodded, waved, and headed for school.

I tucked the handkerchief into my pocket and went on to work. Since I'd started out early, I was at the site long before anyone else. I climbed to the newly finished gallery on the last house, then up to the roof where Frank and Charlie had begun shingling yesterday evening.

I could see the whole city from up there, and recognized a lot of the buildings that Uncle Nate had pointed out on our trip from the train station. St. Patrick's Catholic Church, with its spires still under construction, and Bath Avenue School. The Levy Building on Market and the Tremont Hotel. The twin towers of St. Mary's Cathedral and, of course, the thousands of gray slate roofs.

I turned and looked east, following the curve of the beach toward Bolivar Roads, the great deepwater channel at the end of the island. A large freighter had just emerged from Galveston Bay, making its way through the Roads. The north wind blew great plumes of steam over her bow, and I watched till she became a dark spot on the horizon, all but lost in the wide green gulf. Then I heard voices.

The men were here, and it was time to go to work.

Chapter

8

The north wind had swept clouds into thin wisps across the sky like fine white silk, and other than being hotter than usual, the day was turning out well. Like before, Mr. Farrell put me to work with Josiah and Zach, and again the three of us fell into that indefinable rhythm. Hammers rang, saws rasped, and the hours slipped away.

By evening, I heard a girl's voice and looked over the balcony railing. My heart gave a wild thump and jumped into my throat. The girl was Ella Rose.

She stood below, talking to Henry and Mr. Farrell, but her face looked clouded and serious. Zach and Josiah walked down with me to see what was going on, and Frank and Charlie followed.

"The storm flag went up this morning," Ella Rose said when she saw me. "I wasn't sure if any of you had heard."

Her hair billowed in the strengthening breeze, and

bright tendrils caught on her lashes and in the corner of her mouth.

"Are you planning to work tomorrow, boss?" Henry asked.

Mr. Farrell nodded. "If it rains, we'll work inside."

I glanced at the clouds tumbling in from the northeast. It was a good thing Frank and Charlie had finished the shingling today.

Mr. Farrell squinted toward the sun and checked his watch. "I guess we'll call it a day, boys, and hope for the best tomorrow."

"Are you walking?" I asked Ella Rose.

She nodded. "And you?"

"Every day," I said. "If you don't mind waiting while I put away the tools, I would be happy to keep you company. Josiah goes that way, too."

A startled look swept across Josiah's face. He helped put everything away, then took off north with Zach and his brothers.

"Where are you going?" I called after him, but he either didn't hear or didn't want to hear. I turned to Ella Rose and shrugged. "Want to follow the beach for a few blocks?"

She nodded, and I took her books.

We walked past the Midway and the giant bathhouses where only a few souls braved the waves this evening, riding huge swells that seemed to almost touch the lamps suspended over the surf. There surely wouldn't be any nude bathing beyond the lights tonight. Then it hit me. With a storm coming, there probably wouldn't be any bathing tomorrow, either, of any kind. I glanced at Ella Rose, wondering if she'd already thought of that. Of course, we hadn't made a real date, but even so, it would be a dark disappointment if a whole week passed before I had a chance to see her again.

"The waves look strange, don't they?" she asked.

A strong wind pushed against my back as I looked out over the rough surf. I tried to see what was different, but I hadn't been here long enough to know what was strange and what wasn't.

"Usually, a north wind pushes the tide out, leaving hardly a ripple on the water. Mr. Farrell told me this evening that the whole gulf should be looking so shallow you'd think you could walk all the way to Cuba if you wanted." She shook her head. "That's not happening this time."

I squinted out over the waves, wondering why this north wind was different. "But storms happen here all the time, so they can't be all that bad, can they?"

She shrugged. "About fifteen years ago, a little town not far from here called Indianola was completely washed away, scattered all across the prairie. But everyone says it couldn't happen again, and certainly not here in Galveston. We get storms and overflows all the time, and they never last long or do much damage. It's kind of exciting, really, watching the waves and seeing the water rise up in the streets and yards."

I looked at the way her eyes shone and realized that there was nothing I'd like better than to experience my first island storm with Ella Rose.

We turned back toward Avenue N, passed Ursuline and the Garten Verein, then headed up Thirty-fifth Street. I saw Andy and Will playing on the veranda at Uncle Nate's. I waved, then glanced down the side of the house to the alley, curious to see if Josiah had made it home. He'd stirred something uneasy in me, leaving quick the way he had. I caught a glimpse of him helping Ezra in the garden as we passed by. He'd walked straight home after all. Just not with us.

I said good-bye to Ella Rose at the foot of her stairs, but she insisted that I come up to meet her father. My stomach rolled like one of those giant swells rushing toward the beach. I glanced at my dirty fingernails and scuffed shoes and shook my head. "Another time, maybe, when I haven't been working."

She laughed. "You don't know Daddy. He'd much rather see you grimy from working hard than all spiffy and clean."

I pulled in a deep breath, smoothed my windblown hair, and followed her up the stairs.

She took her books from me, set them on a side table

in the foyer, and dragged me into the parlor. I tossed a quick glance at the piano in the corner, the artwork on the walls, and the family portrait of Ella Rose and her parents sitting on the mantel in a gilded frame.

"Daddy?"

Mr. Covington looked up from his newspaper.

"I'd like you to meet Seth Braeden. He's new to Galveston and already has a fine job working for Mr. Farrell. You remember Mr. Farrell, don't you, Daddy? Henry works for him, too."

Mr. Covington nodded. "So you're a builder, are you, Seth?"

"Yessir," I said, rubbing my sweaty palm against my pants. "At least I'd like to be." I held out my hand, hoping like everything that it was clean enough to shake. "It's a pleasure to meet you, sir." His warm grasp eased my mind somewhat.

Ella Rose gave her father a shiny smile. "I stopped by to see if Henry and the others knew about the storm warning, and Seth was kind enough to see me home."

"Ah, yes. Isaac Cline raised the flag above the Levy Building this morning." He shook his head. "But you know how those weathermen are. Always making a big to-do over every little blow."

I nodded, the last of my concern about the storm finally gone. Even Mr. Covington wasn't worried.

For the next few minutes, he asked the kind of

questions I suppose all newcomers are asked, and I answered the best I could, acutely aware that his impression of me would determine whether I saw his daughter again or not. When we finally said our good-byes, I blew out a relieved breath and headed home. With a storm coming, I might not see Ella Rose again till next weekend. But if her father didn't like me, I might not see her ever again.

When I got home, it appeared that the Vedder children had become the envy of the neighborhood. Their daddy's ragged hearse bumped along behind old gray Whiskers, and a solemn procession of mourners followed, heads bent, hands full of jasmine and oleander blossoms.

I laughed. "Hey, who died?"

Up popped Kate, grinning from behind the hearse's ragged velvet drapery and waving a bunch of jasmine vines at me. "Look at me, Seth!"

I waved back and headed for the stairs. Matt sat sulking on the bottom step beside Lucas, his baseball in his lap.

"They're playing funeral," Lucas grumbled.

Matt huffed his irritation. "Ain't that just about the dumbest thing you ever saw?"

I looked again. They'd pulled Kate from the hearse and laid her in the grass. She lay deathly still while they covered her with flowers.

Something cold and sick squirmed inside me, and I found myself wanting to chase the brats home, grab Kate up, and bring her into the house with me. But I turned my back on the scene instead, and squeezed around Matt and Lucas. "Yeah, pretty dumb, all right," I muttered, and headed upstairs to find my cold supper.

That night I pulled Ella Rose's handkerchief from my pocket. The scent of lilac water still clung to it, making me wonder if her skin smelled as sweet. I folded it, set it on my night table, and turned my thoughts to the storm.

Mr. Covington hadn't been worried at all, but in the dark, the house seemed to creak and sigh more than usual. And when I was very still, I could feel the deep thudding of gulf swells falling upon the beach just blocks away. The shock waves vibrated up the walls, through the floor, and right into my bones.

Chapter

9

I took Broadway to work Saturday morning. The north wind remained brisk, and the dawn sky took on a mother-of-pearl iridescence unlike anything I'd ever seen before. I stumbled more than a few times, foolishly staring at the sky instead of watching where I was going.

I turned south toward the construction site and soon found tidewater over the tops of my shoes. Startled, I searched the faces around me but didn't see a flicker of concern. A light rain swept in, and still people walked to work, trolleys ran, and horses pulled loaded delivery wagons same as always, splashing through the shallow overflow. I glanced down the street to the gulf where great waves broke on the beach, sending showers of white spray into the air. Storms and overflows might be a normal occurrence around here, but I wasn't sure I'd ever get used to it. It made me feel like the whole island was sinking into the sea.

When I got to work, Mr. Farrell was already there on the fourth-house gallery, ignoring the rain, looking out over the beach. I climbed up beside him, and he pointed toward the streetcar trestle strung across the surf. Swells crashed against pilings and across rails, hurling plumes of white spray as high as telephone poles. Farther down, spent waves had already reached the Midway. Fingers of foam raced around the ramshackle restaurants and shops as if searching for something to drag back into the sea.

We watched till everyone arrived, then Mr. Farrell put us to trimming doors and windows inside the first two houses. Concentrating on work wasn't easy, though. Even Zach had a hard time with such a spectacle going on outside.

Streets and yards around us filled with rain and tidewater, yet people trickled in from trolleys, buggies, and on foot. Men in suits, dressed for work, and women gripping the hands of children gathered to see a sight as grand as fireworks on the Fourth of July.

As the morning wore on, the storm increased, and so did the crowds. Streetcars stopped three blocks short of the beach, no longer venturing out over the wild surf, and still people braved the rising water to see the show. Some of them even wore their bathing suits.

Skies darkened. Wind stripped umbrellas inside out and blew hats tumbling toward the surf. A driving rain soaked sightseers' backs and peppered the north side of the house where I'd been working, striking like pebbles against windows and siding.

I heard cries as waves picked up the two-wheeled portable bathhouses and flung them into the row of flimsy buildings that made up the Midway, showering brightly painted pieces of wood over the roofs. Farther down, swells rolled in, one upon the other, exploding against creosoted pilings under the Pagoda and slamming against floor joists with such force, I could feel the gallery railing shudder beneath my hands.

Mr. Farrell shouted from the house next to us. "Looks like it might get worse before it gets better. You boys best get on home."

Zach nodded and waved. We dropped our tools inside the unfinished parlor and headed out into the rain.

"You live pretty far out, don't you, Seth?" Zach asked. "You're welcome to come wait out the storm with us if you want."

I shook my head. "Thanks, but I'll feel better knowing that things are okay at home."

"I guess I would, too." He held up a hand. "Monday morning, then."

I nodded. "I'll be here."

We all struck out in almost knee-deep water, headed toward higher ground—Zach with Frank and Charlie, and Henry with Mr. Farrell. Josiah and I trudged behind them but stopped when we heard excited yells behind us. We turned in time to see the Midway buildings lift on the waves and crash to the ground like kindling. Josiah gave me a stunned look as debris washed toward the shocked crowds. Many people turned to leave, but some stayed on, their faces lit with excitement.

"Let's go!" I yelled over the sound of the surf. Josiah nodded, and we bent our heads into the rain, wading toward the higher ground on Broadway where I hoped we'd have an easier time of getting home.

Rising water and high curbs had turned the south streets into rushing brown rivers, but buggies and drays still moved along them as if overflows were a daily occurrence. Kids floated by on homemade rafts or paddled along in washtubs, bumping into broken tree limbs and odd bits of bobbing lumber. They laughed while wet hair whipped around their faces.

Everywhere I looked I saw tiny green frogs, thousands of them, covering floating debris, sitting on fence posts and porches, and even riding astride a horse's back.

We waded out of the water just one block shy of Broadway and made our way west toward Thirty-fifth Street. It wasn't long before I saw whole families struggling in from the beach roads just like we had, leaving their homes for higher ground. They carried clothing, food, and framed photographs, and ahead of them they pushed muddy kids hugging kittens and puppies to their chests.

"The bay and the gulf have joined!" one of them yelled, pointing to the street.

I looked and saw water rushing in from Galveston Bay on one side and from the gulf on the other. The two seas met in the middle of Broadway, swirling over the wooden paving blocks, and I couldn't help but shudder at the sight. All of Galveston appeared to be under water.

When we reached Twenty-fourth Street, I looked south toward the gulf, trying to keep an eye on the stalking sea. Wild waves rose up like a great hand and wrenched loose the Pagoda's long staircase, sending planks tumbling through the air. With horror I watched the end of one twin building sway and dip into the surf.

I yelled at Josiah, but my words disappeared on the wind. I grabbed his arm, pointed, and we stood together, shoulder to shoulder, mouths gaping, watching the impossible.

Like a wounded Goliath, the great bathhouse shuddered, folded in on its long legs, and collapsed into the sea.

Chapter

10

My heart pounded as hard as the rain while, blocks away, the Pagoda's twin buildings broke apart. Waves flung huge chunks of splintered wood into the air and dashed them into the homes overlooking the gulf.

The staggering truth of what was happening twisted so tight inside me I could hardly breathe. This was far more than the simple storm with overflows that everyone had expected. I stared toward the flooded beach and wondered if there were some who still watched, paralyzed, unable to tear themselves from the horror of seeing their great bathhouses ripped apart by the sea.

Josiah nudged my arm. "We needs to go."

He blinked in the stinging rain, and I nodded, thankful to leave the shattered Pagoda behind. All I wanted now was to get to Uncle Nate's, where I hoped to find Mama, Papa, and the kids, safe and dry.

Over the wind and rain, I heard shouting and dogs

barking. Cows bawled, and chickens squawked with fear as they flapped off to higher roosts. People hurried with us and past us, trying to get home from work or errands, while children still splashed in the rising water, unmindful of the violence that had taken place just blocks away. Horses continued to pull their loads, skirting fallen limbs and no doubt eager for dry barns and fresh hay.

By the time we reached the alley behind Thirty-fifth Street, the wind had shifted slightly to the east. Water swirled around our knees, and thousands of creosoted, wooden pavers swept along Broadway like toy boats. I followed Josiah down the alley to his grandfather's house, and when we found it empty, we checked Uncle Nate's.

Ezra met us at the kitchen door, eyes soft with relief, and though he never said a word to Josiah, it wasn't difficult to sense the great affection that passed between him and his grandson.

"Come in, Mr. Seth," he said. "I'll get towels. You boys is soaked to the bone."

"Is that Seth?" Aunt Julia called from the parlor.

"Yes'm. He be here with Josiah, safe and sound."

"Thank goodness," she said, stepping into the kitchen. "Now if Thomas and Eliza would just get here, too . . . I haven't had an easy breath since all this started. Have you heard?" She looked up at me, eyes full of disbelief. "The bathhouses are gone."

I nodded. "I thought Mama and Papa would be here by now. Didn't they telephone?"

"I haven't heard a word from them, but it's impossible to get a call through now."

I took the towel Ezra held out to me and sat at the table. "They must've decided to stay in the rental."

"Or with one of the neighbors," Aunt Julia added. "The Peeks have a nice sturdy house. Maybe they're there."

"Where're the boys?"

"I gave them a plate of fudge and sent them to their rooms to play."

"And Uncle Nate?"

"He telephoned earlier. He and Ben are trying to save what they can at the lumberyard, and then they'll head home."

I nodded, not wanting to tell her how bad the streets were already. They wouldn't have an easy time of it. I left the towel and walked through to the veranda. Palms and oleanders leaned under the northerly assault, weighted down with water. Rain-darkened slate roofs stretched in every direction as far as I could see, but I figured I could still make it home if I hurried. I glanced down the street toward Ella Rose's house. A light shone from the parlor window.

I told Aunt Julia I'd be right back and ran to check on the Covingtons. I knocked only once. The door opened quickly, and Ella Rose pulled me inside.

"I was watching out the window and saw you coming," she said. "Daddy's still not home, and I can't get through to him on the telephone."

"You're here alone?"

She nodded, eyes dark with worry.

"No sense in waiting here all by yourself. You'd better come back with me."

She scribbled a note for the foyer table and grabbed a hooded cape.

"Ready?" I asked.

With a nod, she slipped her hand in mine, and we splashed back through the knee-deep water to Uncle Nate's.

Aunt Julia stood just inside the door, waiting with towels.

"Her father's not home yet," I said. "I brought her back to wait for him here."

She saw the worry in Ella Rose's face and led her to a chair. "Ben and Mr. Braeden are on their way home, too," she said. "And do remember that Seth and Josiah came through the storm just fine, so we needn't worry too much about those great big men of ours. Now let me get some dry things for you all."

She turned, but I stopped her and held her hand in mine. "I have to go on home, Aunt Julia."

She shook her head hard. "Your mama and papa would never forgive me if I let you go back out in that storm."

"I have to know they're okay," I argued. "They might need me."

She glanced toward the windows, then back at me. "Please, just wait until your Uncle Nate gets here. He'll help you decide what's best."

"I'm sorry, Aunt Julia. I have to go now before the storm gets worse." I handed her the damp towel and saw Josiah standing in the kitchen doorway.

"I'll go with 'im, Miz Braeden," he said.

An ache washed across Ezra's face but quickly disappeared. "See here, Miz Braeden," he soothed. "Don't you worry none. Josiah'll hep look after him."

"I don't know, Ezra." Her fingers twisted in the tail of her apron. "I just don't know."

"Why, these here strapping boys'll do jus' fine. You'll see."

I gave Ezra a grateful glance, kissed Aunt Julia on the cheek, and turned to Ella Rose. "You'll be okay here till your father gets in," I reassured her.

A slight smile lifted the corners of her mouth, and until that moment, I hadn't realized how much I needed to see it.

She reached for my hand. "Please be careful."

I nodded, my heart a jumble of mixed longings. I let my hand slip from hers and followed Josiah to the door. "You'll take good care of them, won't you, Ezra?"

"Yessir," he said. "I surely will."

I turned to Aunt Julia. "I'll see you all tomorrow, and that's a promise."

She bit her bottom lip and gave me an uncertain nod. With a last glance at Ella Rose, I stepped back into the rain.

Josiah and I headed west as fast as we could travel. We waded through knee-deep water at first, but before we were even halfway home, the overflow had risen to the top of my thighs. The wind bursts felt stronger, and the lulls between them shortened. Still, the streets were filled with people who'd been forced to leave their flooding homes. One man floated a bathtub full of children in front of him, trying to reach higher ground. Horses, belly-deep in the rushing brown water, skittered around snakes and snapping wires, dodging broken telephone poles, porches, and cisterns being swept down the streets.

I glanced at Josiah, grateful for his company but shamed that I'd allowed him to come with me. He no doubt needed to be with his grandfather every bit as much as I needed to be with my family. Still, he came.

At Forty-fourth and Avenue S, we came across a house sitting in the middle of the street, an old colonial with tall columns that'd washed off its foundation.

"Butcher Miller's," Josiah shouted over the storm.

A woman carrying a child tried to cross an alley nearby, but the water took them, swirling them away like chips of wood. We watched, hopelessly beyond their reach, while the two just up and disappeared. Josiah squirmed, looking as sick as I felt, but there was nothing we could've done to save them.

Rain hit my skin, stinging like needles shot from cannons, but something even worse had begun to happen. Slate shingles lifted from roofs and flew through the air like hatchets. Bricks, picked up by the increasingly wild wind, struck walls, smashed windows, and knocked people into the swiftly moving water to drown.

A man buckled in front of us and Josiah plunged in after him. I helped wrestle them up from the water, but the man's head leaned at an impossible angle and blood gushed over his shoulder. Josiah stared at me, rain streaming down his face, eyes full of horror. The man's neck had been nearly severed by flying slate.

I wrenched the dead man from Josiah's arms, and the brown water snatched him up, swirled him into an eddy, then swept him away.

Still, Josiah couldn't seem to move. Splintered lumber swept past us, and I grabbed it up. "Like this!" I shouted at him, showing him how to hold a wide board against the airborne assault. I shoved it into his hands, grabbed another for myself, and we plunged ahead, holding our boards like shields till I stepped into a hole washed out by the swirling current.

I flailed for footing while muddy water swept over my head and rushed into my mouth and nose. Feeling Josiah's hand, I latched on to him, and he pulled me up, gasping and sputtering.

I gagged and coughed up foul-tasting saltwater, and when the wind gusted again, we had to duck the debris flying through the air and sweeping down the flooded streets. Josiah shoved his board in front of me, protecting my head and shoulders, then grabbed another for himself.

As soon as I caught my breath, we started out again, but by then, I wondered if we'd ever make it. I wondered, too, if I'd ever have a chance to make things right with Papa. I should've never been so angry with him. He only wanted me to have what he'd been denied. And Mama. She cooked and cleaned up after us without a single complaint, while I never bothered to hide my resentment over the way she leaned on me.

I remembered Matt, that glimpse I'd gotten of the generous man he was becoming, and the appreciation

I'd seen on Lucas's face. Even at ten, he already knew what was important in this life.

And Kate.

I closed my eyes against the driving rain. I smelled her sweet watermelon breath, felt her little hands around my neck, heard her baby voice saying, "I waited and waited."

The memory caught in my throat, and I felt like I'd stepped into another deep hole.

Time seemed suspended, circling our struggle, watching for weakness. I glanced at Josiah, truly sorry I'd gotten him into this. My legs ached from fighting the current, my whole body felt bruised and battered, and I knew it had to be the same for him.

All around us people fell, struck down by flying slate, brick, or shutters. Others drowned, knocked off their feet and carried under by the broken roofs, galleries, or privies that swept down the street faster than a man could run. Water swirled around my hips, leaving me powerless to offer aid and weak with the thought that, at any moment, either one of us could disappear beneath the swift brown river and be gone.

Chapter

11

Josiah stumbled, and I hooked a drenched arm through his. He grabbed it, and we leaned into each other, pushing hard through the wind and rising water. Slate and shattered lumber hit all around us. Submerged objects struck my legs, sharp and piercing one minute, fleshy and stomach-churning the next. Then, gratefully, I'd feel them slide away, caught up in the current again.

During a short lull, I stopped to get my bearings, squinting through the rain, and at last, hope pounded in my chest. "Look!" I shouted. "There!"

Josiah pulled hard at my arm, dragging me toward the house. We struggled past the fence, across the yard, and took the stairs up and out of the water. My legs felt like tree stumps, and when I closed the door behind us, my ears rang.

"Mama! Papa!" I yelled.

I stumbled from room to room but found no one—

nothing till I saw a note tacked to my bedroom door. I tore it off and read Papa's hurried scrawl out loud to Josiah.

Seth,
Gone to Nate's. Hope to find you safe there. If not, trust you will seek sturdier shelter with Peeks or Vedders. God be with you.

Papa

I stared at the note, picturing Mama, Papa, and the kids with slate flying around their heads and debris washing down flooded streets toward them like freight trains.

Had I passed them out there and not realized it?

The woman swept away—I hadn't seen her face.

The child—was the hair dark? Was it Kate?

I closed my eyes till the sick wave of fear eased. Still shaky, knees weak, I walked back through the house. Dinner sat on the table, uneaten. A cake and a pitcher of boiled custard waited on the stove. Matt's baseball lay in the seat of a chair, and beside it, a small handful of wilted jasmine.

Kate's funeral flowers.

I picked up the brown blossoms, stuffed them in

one pocket, and poked the ball in the other. Then I noticed that my pants were torn and my leg oozed blood. I looked at Josiah, at all his scrapes and cuts. We'd had a rough time of it, but we'd made it.

"So they's with Mister Braeden?" he asked.

"I hope so," I said, staring at the note.

"So we needs to get to the Vedders'."

I shook my head. "Aunt Julia said the Peeks have a real sturdy house. Might be better there."

Josiah cocked his head and looked at me. "My bones is sayin' Vedders."

I gave him a surprised look, and he laughed at me, easylike, his eyes full of something warm I'd only sensed before. I felt it sifting through me, easing my aches and worry. "Okay," I said finally, grinning at him. "The Vedders it is, then."

We turned, headed for the door, when the window exploded. I ducked, covering my head while glass shot past Josiah, clear across the house. He caught a piece in his forehead, and blood streamed down his face and into his eyes. I pulled the three-inch sliver from his skin, ripped a kitchen towel lengthwise, and tied it around his head.

Wind whipped through the open window, pummeling the walls and ceilings till cracks raced around the plaster.

"Let's get out of here before the roof goes!" I shouted.

He nodded, and we scrambled down the stairs, back into the water and howling wind.

We must've looked like drowned rats when the Vedders opened their door to us, but they were a sight, too, dressed in woolen bathing suits. Mrs. Vedder insisted we have some warm broth, and I gratefully accepted, collapsing into a ladder-back chair at the kitchen table. Josiah hesitated, his hands poked deep inside his wet pockets till Mr. Vedder pulled out a chair for him, too.

"Sit down, Josiah. At times like these we can't stand on ceremony."

Josiah nodded and mumbled, "Yessir. Thank you, sir."

The house shuddered in the wind, and while we downed our bowls of broth, Mr. Vedder talked to us about the storm.

"This house isn't as well-built as the Richard Peek house," he said. "I figure if it starts to break up, we'll make a human chain, and you boys can follow us down the fence line to the Peeks'."

I nodded and glanced at Josiah, wondering if his bones had anything to say about that.

Five-year-old Katherine tugged at my shirt sleeve. "Where's Kate?" she asked. "Didn't she come with you?"

I shook my head. "She's with her mama and papa."

"Are they at home?"

"No, they're all safe and sound at my uncle's house," I said, praying it was so.

"Well, I sure wish she was here. No one will play with me. Not Jacob or Allen, not even Lola. They all say I'm too little."

She wandered off, and I turned my attention back to the storm.

The Vedder house had been tightly shuttered, but through a broken slat, I could see all the way to the swollen gulf. It was a staggering sight—home after home looking like tiny islands surrounded by angry sea, like they'd been built in the middle of an ocean. The ones closest to the gulf were gone, splintered and swept away or slammed against others, waiting for the next wave.

Farther out, a big gray wall of water, like an army of elephants, moved slow and sure toward the island. It was held somewhat at bay by the northeast wind, but I couldn't help but wonder what it would mean to all of us if the wind shifted to the south.

I blinked the sick thought away and kept an eye on the water in the yard. It soon swamped the four-foot fence, and I knew it was just a matter of time before waves broke up the closest row of houses and sent them slamming into us.

The house began to fill with people, some whose

homes had already come apart and some who feared theirs would soon follow. Mr. and Mrs. Mason came with their children, along with a number of soldiers from Fort Crockett, till there must've been fifty of us gathered in the front hall. Josiah and one of the soldiers, Private Orville Billings, helped Mr. Vedder remove closet doors, then we all helped nail them crossways to reinforce the windows and front entry.

The storm roared and buffeted the house. The women sat on the stairs, taking care not to show their fear to the children. Katherine, content at last to have playmates, sat under the staircase, sharing her new gray kitten with Francesca and Kearny, Jr.

Josiah and I had just settled on the floor near the kids when I felt a movement. My vision blurred, and a wave of queasiness hit me. Out of the corner of my eye, I saw a small table slide a few feet across the floor. I stared at it, confused for a moment, then felt the whole house rise and rock like a ship at sea. Shocked cries sounded all around me. We were afloat!

Timbers groaned and cracked as the house washed off its six-foot foundation. Seconds later, we hit the ground with a jaw-shattering jolt. My ears popped, and water gushed into the house so fast I didn't have time to get to my feet. I kicked and groped my way to the surface, grabbing for Josiah to make sure he would make it, too, but he was already up, fishing Kearny, Jr., from the murky water. I grappled for Francesca and handed her, dripping, to her panicky mother, who had been forced to flee farther up the stairs. Lola and Allen popped up, then Jacob, his bathing suit nearly ripped off him. Private Billings pulled Katherine out, sputtering and crying, "Papa! Papa!" Mr. Vedder took her on his back, but the water quickly rose again. I pulled her from him and set her on the stairs, only to hear her cry once more—this time for her kitten.

Mr. Vedder pulled the soaked and clawing fur ball from the water and tossed it on the stairs. Mrs. Mason, caught unawares, jumped, shrieking, "Rat!" and slung it back. There must've been a dozen of us men, all up to our necks in cold dark water, scrambling to save that shivering gray kitten once again.

Dark closed over us, and still the house shook with each violent burst of wind. Waves crashed through broken windows. Huge beams from the newly constructed barracks at Fort Crockett thudded against the walls. We helped Mr. Vedder renail the closet doors, loosened by the settling of the house, then stood with arms stretched through the cracks where the front door had once been, pushing away beams and timbers during each lull. Others stood near windows, doing the same, fighting to keep the house from being battered into kindling.

A sound loud as a freight train roared over our heads.

I heard a great cracking and splintering, and when it stopped, the house listed to the north and rain poured down the stairs. Mrs. Vedder checked and reported back.

"The roof over the two east bedrooms is gone," she said with surprising calm.

She moved the women and children farther up the flooded stairs and finally into the bathroom. I stayed behind with Josiah, helping Mr. Vedder ward off the battering rams till the water rose so high we had to give up. Our arms were torn, full of splinters and glass, but none were hurt as bad as poor Mr. Vedder. We took him to the bathroom, where maybe fifteen people had gathered, mostly women and children.

Faces turned to us, and candlelight flickered in eyes that were empty of everything but fear. The smaller children lay in the big white tub, bundled in bedspreads, urged to sleep. Jacob, his ripped bathing suit discarded on the floor, didn't look too happy about having to wear Lola's petticoat.

I shut the door, leaving Mrs. Vedder to wrap her husband's arms and hands with what was left of the clean toweling, and sat in the dark hall with Josiah and the rest of the men.

No one spoke. We shivered from the cold and rocked with each explosive blast of wind and water, but it was the eerie lulls that finally made me cover my ears.

In brief, crystal seconds, I heard the crunching of houses breaking apart, the terrified bawling of animals, the faraway cries of people praying and pleading for help. I thought of Mama, Papa, and the kids, which quickly brought me back to the woman I'd seen just hours ago, whisked down the flooded alley, clinging to her child.

A choking ache washed over me, filling my eyes and knotting in my throat.

Oh, heaven, please help them—and me as well. For in my selfishness, I continued to pray that the woman and child hadn't been Mama and Kate.

Chapter

～ 12 ～

Floating furniture thudded against the first-floor ceiling right below me, and still the water rose. It sloshed around me while I sat in the dark hall, elbows propped on my knees, arms wrapped around my ears. I speculated, considering my position near the east bedrooms, what I would do if I heard that final great crack, that signal to all of us that the house was breaking apart. I'd likely be crushed under its weight, or maybe thrown right through the missing roof, immersed in muddy, pitch-black water, and tangled in debris to drown. There seemed to be no real hope for any of us.

Like the cold, fear crawled along my skin and soaked right through to my bones. I shivered so hard my teeth rattled. Josiah moved closer and I leaned into him, grateful to share his small portion of warmth.

I think I might've dozed some then, but if so, it was a brief and fretful escape with the wind howling and the house rocking so. Then voices—close voices—cut through my weariness and brought me to my feet.

"It's coming from the west side," Mr. Mason said.

Josiah and I hurried after him into the windy west bedroom, crawling through water and across an overturned bureau and spilled drawers. A light shone through a broken window, and I stared at the pale glow, unable to fathom its meaning at first. A full moon stared back at me, a lantern suspended in a black sky, and the sweet realization sunk in. Even though the wind still howled like wolves, its teeth, exposed by moonlight, didn't look quite as sharp as they had.

Waves crashed against the wall and in through the second-story window, drenching us badly but bringing the voices even closer.

"How many?" I asked, blinking from the salt spray.

Mr. Mason leaned across the sill. "Four, I think." He stretched out his arm. "Here! Quick, give me your hand!" he shouted.

He pulled Mr. and Mrs. Collum from an upturned roof and dragged them through the window. Then Mrs. Longineau shoved her six-week-old son into my arms while she and her husband scrambled from their wind-tossed raft just in time. It scraped against the house and was swept away.

"Was there anyone else?" Mr. Mason asked.

Mr. Longineau shook his head and pulled the back of his wife's skirt up over her bare shoulders. Wind and debris had shredded much of their clothing and the poor woman shivered from the cold.

Sobs poured from Mrs. Collum as she told us how their house had broken apart and their cherished pets had to be abandoned.

"The parrots kept calling, 'Mama, Mama,' and we couldn't do a thing to save them."

Mr. Mason tried to comfort her, but it was the baby that troubled me most. He was soaked through and lay limp in my arms. I wrapped his cold hands in mine, shook him a bit, and studied him in the pale moonlight. He didn't stir. Hugging him close, I led the way back down the hall to the bathroom.

Mrs. Vedder must've recognized the voices, for she stood in the doorway, waiting, faint candlelight sputtering behind her, arms held wide in welcome.

Full of dread, I handed the baby back to his mother. She checked him tenderly, then hugged him close while tears rolled down her face.

"Oh, Florence," she whispered to Mrs. Vedder, "he's gone." She slowly rocked back and forth. "My sweet little Tom is gone."

Mrs. Vedder grabbed a shaving mirror and held it close to the baby's nose. We watched and waited.

A tiny moist circle formed on the glass, and I heard

Mrs. Longineau suck in a surprised breath. Grateful tears flooded her cheeks.

"He's going to be fine, darlin', you'll see." Mrs. Vedder patted her shoulder. "We just need something warm to wrap him in."

She squeezed past the crowd that had gathered around the door, dropped to her knees, and crawled into the battered west bedroom. She returned shortly, her hair blown askew, and in her hand she gripped a cracked bottle of cordial. Under her arm, she'd tucked a knitted woolen petticoat taken from the overturned bureau. She quickly stripped the baby of his wet clothing, wrapped him in the dry petticoat, and placed Katherine's purring kitten beside him for added warmth. Then she handed the baby back to Mrs. Longineau and promptly poured the cordial into an empty shaving mug.

"Strain it through your teeth in case there's any broken glass and put it drop by drop into little Tom's mouth."

Mrs. Longineau nodded, and while she did as she was told, we waited.

When I sat back down in the hall with the other men, I noticed that the water had receded. It was too dark to tell by how much, but the floor no longer sloshed beneath me.

I rested my hand on Matt's baseball bulging in my pocket, and Josiah and I leaned against the soaked and crumbling plaster. My thoughts drifted from little Tom to Thirty-fifth Street, from the faces of my family to Ella Rose, but they always ended up in the alley behind Butcher Miller's house, reaching for the woman and her child.

Chapter

~ 13 ~

A sound stirred me from my sleep, a soft cry that finally hit such a demanding note, I jerked upright. I heard relieved laughter coming from the bathroom, then from the men around me. Little Tom was awake and hungry.

I laughed then, too, and for the first time noticed that Tom's howls were the only ones I heard. The wind had died. Someone forced open the swollen doors in the hallway, and through the missing roof in the sloping east bedrooms, I saw faint, purple signs of coming daybreak.

The storm was over.

All around me I felt men rise in the dark hall— soldiers from Fort Crockett, neighbors I barely knew, and some whose faces I'd never seen before yesterday. As if Tom's cry had been the final call back to the real world, we pushed ourselves up from the buckled floor, then pulled up our neighbor beside us. Women slowly crept from the bathroom, a few with candles, some with children hugged against their legs, but not a word was spoken.

Josiah helped me to my feet, and in the flickering candlelight, I could see the relief in his face. I straightened the makeshift bandage on his head, stretched my stiff back and sore legs, and heard a hoarse voice calling from outside.

"Anybody in there?"

Surprise crackled around me. We hurried down the stairs, waded through several feet of foul-smelling muddy water, and ripped away what was left of the closet doors we'd nailed up.

There must've been a dozen of us crowded around the splintered doorway, staring in shocked silence at a man standing in the gloom, stark naked except for a piece of mattress ticking.

"It's me," the man said. "Munn."

When we finally came to our senses, Mr. Mason drew Captain Munn up the stairs, out of the muddy water, and into the candlelight.

The poor man collapsed on the upper landing, telling us how his house had broken apart all around him and how he'd clung to a mattress all night in the raging waves and rain. Then he looked at us with eyes dark and bottomless, swimming with the deepest sorrow I'd ever beheld.

"They're gone," he said quietly.

His words betrayed no emotion, and yet tears rolled down his face.

"My wife, her mother, my house." He slowly shook his head. "Everyone, everything. Gone."

I'd never seen such desolation in a man's face, and a wave of fear for what I might find at Uncle Nate's rose inside me.

Mrs. Mason brought a rag and tried to clean mud from the captain's cuts, and Mrs. Vedder, who'd found a spare shirt and pants, squeezed around the crowd on the landing and set the small stack of clothing beside him.

He stared at it for a long moment, then offered a simple "Thank you kindly."

It was then that I saw his bleak situation fully. That stack of clothing was all he had in this world. I looked around me, from face to face, and saw the same fear in almost every eye. Maybe none of us would end up with any more than the clothes on our backs, but what tore at my heart most was the misery our lives would become if we had no family left, either.

Mr. Mason gave the captain a pat on the shoulder, squeezed past him, and headed back down the stairs. Though it still wasn't light enough to see much, he was determined to climb through a north window to see how his house had fared. While he was gone, others decided to leave, too, wading into the dim, battered landscape, anxious to know the fate of battalions, friends, and family. I wanted to go, too, but Josiah hesitated.

"Best we wait till we got us some light 'fore we gets into all that mud."

He was right, of course. Water was still draining back into the gulf. It would be much easier and safer if we waited just a while longer.

When Mr. Mason got back, faces turned toward him, eager for news of what he'd seen. He handed Mrs. Mason a tin of sardines and a bottle of beer.

"They were in the only corner left standing of our brick storeroom, sitting on a shelf like God himself had put his hand over them." He laughed at the absurdity of it. "Imagine that, Virginia. Sardines and beer."

Mrs. Mason reached for her husband's hand and waited to hear the rest.

"It's all gone," he whispered, "like Captain Munn said. Everything, Virginia. Just gone."

She slowly shook her head. "Not everything, Kearny. We're all still here." She pulled the key off the sardine can. "And now we've got sardines and beer, too."

Uneasy laughter skittered around the hallway while she opened the tin and the bottle of beer and passed them to what was left of our group. I took a small portion, just enough to make me realize how hungry and thirsty I really was.

"The water in the cistern is salty," Mr. Mason said. "We'll have to do without until we can get back to town."

Heads nodded around me, but worry showed in every face. I couldn't even guess what we might find as we headed toward town. Every cistern left standing could very well be ruined.

When the darkness over the east bedrooms had brightened, we eased back down the stairs and sloshed through the stinking mud to see for ourselves what the storm had done.

Under a soft Sunday-morning sky, I stood in knee-deep water, staring. The Vedder house, swept off its foundation and listing to the north, was one of only three houses left standing. I looked toward Avenue R where our rental had been and saw only more debris and muddy water.

Wreckage spread in every direction. I saw piles of broken chairs and cooking pots, baby buggies and shredded bedding, soaked books and photographs, and all of it lay half-buried in the foulest mud I'd ever smelled. A sickening sludge, churned up from the bowels of the gulf, had painted most everything dark gray. I turned slowly, trying to take in the dismal landscape, already yearning for something green, but not a leaf or a blade of grass could be seen anywhere.

"Papa!" Jacob called. "Where are the Peeks?"

We all looked to the west where the Peeks' house had been, but there was nothing left, not even the foundation. Mr. and Mrs. Peek, six children, and two servants were gone.

Just gone.

"And it was to their house," Mr. Vedder whispered, "that I would've taken you all for refuge."

The staggering truth of what might've been hit us all.

I saw Josiah staring past me, a wretched look on his face, and turned, trying to see what had caught his attention. A big black retriever lay almost buried in mud. Flies buzzed around his eyes and gaping mouth, but it appeared to be the piece of blue gingham floating next to the dog that had carved the painful look on Josiah's face. Puzzled, I looked closer, and finally understood. A battered, muddy arm protruded from a sleeve. What once must've been sunshine hair now lay matted and strewn across a porcelain face, partially concealing glassy blue eyes and pale lips.

Josiah stepped back, but I couldn't move. I couldn't stop staring at that tangled, yellow hair.

"It ain't her," Josiah whispered.

I pulled in a ragged breath. I knew it wasn't, even if my heart didn't, but having seen one body, now I saw them everywhere. I counted three more, and while others checked them, trying to figure out who they were, Josiah pulled me back into the house.

"We needs to wait a bit longer," he said softly, "for the water to go on down."

I nodded again, too sick to speak, and crawled up the stairs, out of the greasy dark mud to wait. We could do nothing else. It was impossible to bury a single soul with so much muddy water around.

With each hour that passed, the day grew warmer and the smell grew worse. The mud pushed ashore from the bottom of the gulf had its own unbearable stench, but with such intense heat, I feared something even less tolerable would soon drift in through the broken windows.

I buried my face in my hands, unable to get the picture of the girl in blue gingham out of my head. Every time I thought of her, I saw only Ella Rose.

Chapter

⁓ 14 ⁓

By midmorning, sweat crawled all over me, trickling down my scalp and back. The children whined for water, and fear pulled at every face. We couldn't stay in this battered house any longer. Like everyone else, I was thirsty, too, but it was the worry that pushed me back outside. I needed to know if my family was safe.

The sun had risen in a bright sky like nothing had happened, but stifling odors from mud and death said otherwise. I tried to remember the scent of fresh-cut lumber, or clover, or jasmine, or Mama's bread browning in the oven—anything that might cut through the sick air that coated my throat and the back of my tongue.

Nothing helped.

I avoided looking at the lifeless limbs and faces, the animals that would soon be swelling in the heat, and concentrated on getting my bearings. Not a single street or landmark was visible above the ruin that lay around us.

From the Vedders' second-floor window, I'd seen a wide ridge of debris off to the east. It looked to be several stories high, as if a great broom had swept up everything in its path and left it there in a twisted heap. I'd wondered then how many people had huddled in those shattered houses last night, and now I wondered how many might still be there, twined inside the wreckage.

Though the water had receded somewhat, we finally decided that making our way to the beach might be best, where the rubble wasn't quite so high and the salt air sweeter. Farther down, we might see an easier path through the ridge of debris that lay between us and town.

We must've been a strange-looking bunch, slowly moving over the muddy gray remains of what was left of so many lives. Captain Munn had gathered up his pants with a piece of cording, like a kid in his big brother's hand-me-downs, and Mrs. Longineau, holding little Tom, walked beside her husband with the back of her dress pulled up over her bare shoulders, shredded underskirts rustling behind her in the breeze. All the Vedders still wore their woolen bathing suits, except for Jacob. He didn't complain, but he'd developed a permanent scowl at having to face the world in his sister's petticoat. The rest of us—the Masons and Collums, Private Billings, Josiah and I—took turns carrying Francesca, Katherine, and her kitten, following along in our tattered and grimy clothing.

The beach appeared torn and uneven, and we quickly realized that the wet sand we were walking on had once held homes. Pounding waves had eaten away at the island, pulling several hundred feet of shoreline into the gulf. I remembered Saint Mary's Orphanage and the ten sisters who took care of more than ninety children there. I glanced behind me, hoping to see the two large dormitories that housed them all still standing beyond the dunes, but they were gone.

When we passed what was left of Fort Crockett, we found several dead soldiers from Battery O who must've been caught in the barracks when they fell. Private Billings laid them out, side by side, to wait for the burial parties that were sure to come. "If not for some all-wise providence that directed me to your house last night," he told Mr. Vedder, "this would've been me."

We carried the smaller kids on our shoulders while we picked our way over piles of splintered wood. Sometimes we sidestepped the deep, water-filled holes washed out by the storm, and sometimes we had no choice but to wade through them, pushing aside dead chickens and dogs, broken toys and furniture.

I tried like everything to not look into the eyes of the dead, though I could feel them tugging at me. I didn't want to think about what they'd suffered. I didn't want to consider that Mama, Papa, and the kids might've met the same fate. It was too much misery to carry with me.

Instead, I fixed my attention on watching my step, and I was doing okay till we came upon a nun from Saint Mary's Orphanage. She lay facedown, half-buried in the muddy beach, her torn black habit billowing above her in the wind like death's own flag.

Mr. Mason dropped to his knees, digging with his hands to free her, and the rest of us men fell around him. We pulled the wet sand away and turned her over. Slender fingers gripped cording that had been tied around her waist, but the other end still lay buried. We dug harder and found a small child tethered to her. Then another. And another.

I heard gasps behind us, whispered prayers and muffled weeping. We laid them out, ten bodies strung together like pearls at the edge of the sea.

I tried to turn away, but I couldn't seem to tear my eyes from the child closest to me. She was small, like Kate. I brushed damp sand from her cheeks and dark lashes and fought hard to choke back the despair knotting in my throat and stinging at my eyes.

I finally turned to Josiah, who sat with his elbows on his knees, his gritty hands around his head, and I was gratefully lost for a moment in the sight of white sand glistening in his black hair. It didn't seem possible that such simple beauty could exist side by side with the mind-numbing sorrow around us.

Mrs. Mason pulled her husband to his feet. "We'll have to leave them," she said.

Everyone nodded except for Captain Munn. He slowly turned, squinting at the wreckage, searching. There'd been no sign of his wife or her mother, and I could see the longing in his eyes, the questions, the ache of not knowing.

I moved closer. "We'll help you watch for them," I whispered.

He nodded, ducked his head, and continued picking his way down the debris-strewn beach.

I turned my back on the nun and her nine charges, set Francesca on my shoulders, and followed, wading through ankle-deep muddy water and big holes washed out by the current.

Death lay everywhere. I feared that hundreds, maybe thousands, of lives might've been taken by the storm. Flies swarmed, and buzzards circled high over horses and cows already swelling in the heat, over men and women half-buried in mud or tangled in barbed wire and splintered timber. Many lay near naked, rocking back and forth in the surf, their clothing shredded, ripped from their bodies by all the debris. Some still grasped the hands of small children, but I knew better than to look into their eyes.

I walked on, my growing numbness a small but welcome barrier to the horror around us, and after a while, someone behind me said, "I wonder how the Edwardses came through." Another said, "And the Wrens; they had five little ones, you know."

No one answered.

"Do you think Captain Minor could've gotten out in time?" Mrs. Collum asked. "He lived so close to the beach, and he was all alone, with his family in Virginia for the summer." And then, as if she already knew the answer, she added, "He felt so safe inside that concrete wall he built around his place."

Mrs. Vedder, far ahead, waded into a hole and stepped onto a barrel half-concealed by muddy water. She sank up to her chin, floundered, and grasped at something floating nearby. The body of a small colored boy rolled under her arm, and the steadfast strength she'd shown throughout the storm gave way.

We hauled her sobbing from the murky water, and she collapsed at our feet, crying, "Charles, oh please, please pull him out."

Mr. Vedder, his hands still bandaged, reached for the boy and managed to drag him from the hole before any of us could help.

Jacob backed away, a whole new look of despair on his face. "It's Toby," he whispered.

Allen nodded. "It's him all right."

I looked closer at the young boy, remembering the way his face had shone when Matt let him throw the fly ball back to Jacob. Had that really been only four days ago?

We stood there, staring. There was no light in Toby's eyes now.

My hand went to the bulge inside my pocket. I hesitated, running my thumb over the stitching, thinking of Matt, but only for a moment. I pulled out the baseball and kneeled beside Toby.

Understanding flickered in Jacob's and Allen's faces, but Josiah's eyes were full of questions. I pushed the ball into the boy's stiff fingers and stepped back. When I glanced again at Josiah, I saw tears.

No one said a word. One by one, they stumbled on, and Josiah and I followed.

I kept a close watch on the ridge of debris off to our left, wondering where Thirty-fifth Street was. It had to be nearby; we'd been walking for hours. Josiah and I took a guess at the location, and, rather than traveling on to look for an easier path, we said our good-byes.

We thanked the Vedders, but I couldn't muster enough words to express my true feelings. A nod, a wish for a loved one's safety, was all I could manage. I stood for a moment, hesitant to leave the people who had become a lifeline to us, but it was they who finally turned and headed farther down the beach.

Josiah and I put the gulf behind us and pushed north toward the mountain that lay between us and our families. The closer we got, the larger it loomed, till we stood at the base of a ridge that rose near twenty feet high.

With the wind at our backs, we reached out, groping our way across the twisted wreckage. My feet rested on broken telephone poles and wagon wheels; my hands fell on clothing and veranda railings; and I wondered with each foot we climbed what might lay beneath this rubble. How many souls?

Josiah, with his long limbs, moved ahead and disappeared over the top. When I caught up with him, he was standing on the corner of a piano wedged tight in the debris. I stood beside him and tried to get my bearings.

The two-story-high ridge was at least a hundred feet across at the base and appeared to wrap around the entire heart of the city. The houses and buildings left standing on this side tilted crazily, and many lay tumbled topsy-turvy, kicked over like toy blocks. Farther north, close to the bay, ships sat askew on land and in water, as if they'd been tossed into the air and left to fall. I looked toward Thirty-fifth Street, which I figured lay just west of us, but couldn't make out much. I couldn't tell if Uncle Nate's house still stood or not.

"We needs to go," Josiah said.

I turned for a last glance at the beach. From my twenty-foot perch I could see for miles, but I couldn't fathom a guess at how many blocks had been swept clean away. There appeared to be nothing standing south of Avenue N. And beneath my feet, twisted into an endless ridge, lay everything—thousands of homes, including the four we'd been working on, the Midway, the giant bathhouses, even trolleys.

Turning my back on the impossible sight, I contemplated a path down, past the sharp slate and splintered wood. Wind whipped at the torn clothing around my feet and whistled around my ears, then I heard something else. My heart thumped. A voice?

Josiah must've heard it, too, because he stopped and turned to look at me.

The weak cry came again, but this time I made out the words. "Can you hear me?" it asked.

A girl's voice. I looked beneath my feet, and the horror of what might be swelled inside me like another storm.

"She be under us," Josiah whispered, dropping to his knees.

I kneeled beside him. "Where are you?" I called, then closed my eyes and listened closely.

"Here," she said weakly. "I can see . . . your leg."

Her breathy voice sounded parched and raspy. I searched the jagged dark openings around me, frantic for a glimpse of her, but couldn't see far enough inside. I began tugging, jerking, ripping at twisted lumber, pulling out dead kittens and broken mirrors, tree limbs and table legs, sending it all tumbling down the ridge. Josiah worked beside me, adding his strength to mine, but large timbers lay twined so tight, finally nothing would budge. It would take dozens of saws to get through it. And time. Perhaps more time than she had.

I fell back, and Josiah did, too, his face streaked with tears and sweat. I hung my head, and for a moment, my whole body shook with sobs.

When I caught my breath, I felt the weight of Josiah's hand on my shoulder. He put a finger to his lips. "Listen," he whispered.

"Please, mister . . . don't cry," the girl pleaded. "I just want . . . to give you . . . my name."

I leaned over the narrow crack, searching the dark for a movement, just one glimpse of her face. "We'll get help," I called.

"I don't want to die . . . without someone . . . knowing my name."

I shoved my hand into the crack, pushing, straining,

desperate to touch her. "We'll find saws; we'll get you out."

"Please, mister . . . I'm Sarah . . . Sarah Louise Ellison."

Her fragile voice ripped at my heart and tangled my breath. I didn't want to just remember her name. I wanted her out.

"Tell her," Josiah begged, his face twisted and tormented. "You has to tell her."

Tears dripped onto my pants in perfect dark circles while I fought for breath enough to speak. "We'll remember, Sarah Louise Ellison," I said finally, sobs choking my words. "Both of us. We'll remember."

Josiah stood and reached for my arm, but I jerked away. My head fell onto my knees. I couldn't leave her yet.

He let me be for a moment, and when he reached out again, I let him pull me to my feet. He placed a jagged piece of mirror above her prison so we could find her again and started down the ridge.

"We'll remember, Sarah Louise Ellison!" I shouted, picking my way down. "And we'll be back!"

Chapter

~ 15 ~

Climbing down from the ridge seemed more difficult than going up. One blunder and we'd end up sliding across the broken slate and glass that stuck out everywhere. It was slow going, and before we were even halfway down, I heard another faint call, a man's voice this time. I stopped and listened.

Josiah tugged at my arm. "We can't hep 'im, Mister Seth. We needs saws, lots of 'em."

I jerked free of his hand, angry at our mounting helplessness, then glared at him. "My name is *not* Mr. Seth. It's just plain ol' Seth."

He stared at me, eyes weary, brimming with misery. "Not for me, it ain't," he said and continued down the ridge.

His words sucked the air right out of me, leaving me almost too weak to move, but I recognized the truth in them. The very people who went out of their way to make sure I made something of myself, like Papa, Uncle Nate, even Mr. Farrell, were the same ones who kept Josiah right where he was.

What I'd asked of him was impossible.

I heard another weak call from deep in the debris, and it propelled me down. I searched the wreckage ahead for help, and not far from us, I saw a half dozen men loading bodies onto wagons.

"We need help!" I called, long before they could hear us well.

An older man with a gray beard turned to watch while we struggled across the muddy ruins toward him.

"People are trapped back there. We need saws!"

They continued to stare but never offered a word.

"I *said*," yelling louder, "there are people back there, trapped, still alive!" I pointed behind me, breathing hard. "I heard them calling for help."

The bearded man nodded slowly. "We heard you, son."

"We ain't got no saws," another man said, pulling a dirty rag from his back pocket.

I felt an angry heat building inside me, and my glare bounced from one set of hollow eyes to another. "So we'll find some," I hissed.

Pain swept across the bearded man's face. He hung his head, pulled in a breath, and when he looked up again, the grief I'd glimpsed only a moment ago had been veiled. "Don't worry, son," he said. "Go on home. We'll take care of those people."

"No, sir." I shook my head hard. "I made a promise."

The man with the dirty rag mopped sweat from his neck. "We already told you boys," he said quietly, "we ain't got no saws."

The rest of the men shifted uneasylike, avoiding my eyes.

"We're doing all we can, son," the bearded man said.

I stared past them to the wagon, to the pile of bodies, the muddied arms and legs, already stiff under the hot sun, and just stood there till Josiah backed away, his head bobbing.

"Thank you, sir," he said to them. "Mister Seth here sure do 'preciates all you is doing."

They nodded, and Josiah pulled me away.

"The man be right," he whispered. "We needs to get home."

"I can't, Josiah. I promised her."

"Yessir, I knows that, but the girl, she already sees how things really is."

I stood there while the hot sun beat down on us, breathing in the terrible odor of mud and death, and squinted up at him.

"My mama tole me right 'fore she died last winter

that angels whispered to her and showed her heaven's own gate. She *knew* she be crossing over real soon."

I peered toward the ridge, trying to make sense of what he was saying. It was true the girl hadn't asked for help. She'd asked only that we remember her name.

The shard of mirror caught the sun, and I flinched from the glare.

"So she knew?" I whispered.

Josiah nodded, and the heavy truth of it slowed my heart till I thought I might die right there with her.

Josiah waited, but I knew I couldn't go home. Not yet.

"I can't leave her," I said.

Sweat trickled down his forehead, and he wiped it away with the back of his sleeve. "I knows," he said, squinting against the sun.

I headed back to the ridge, and without a word, Josiah followed. We began the slow climb, but this time I heard no voices. Not one. I reached the broken mirror and kneeled over the opening. "Sarah Louise!" I shouted. "We're back, like we promised."

Josiah kneeled beside me, listening.

"Sarah," I called again. "Sarah Louise Ellison!"

Wind whistled over the ridge.

I glanced at Josiah, afraid to even breathe, and he hung his head.

Leaning close over the opening, I called again.

And again.

Chapter

~ 16 ~

I sat on the ground, staring up at the broken mirror, not remembering the climb down at all. Josiah let me be for a short while, then pulled me to my feet and led me stumbling toward home. Hot wind gusted around my ears, billowed scattered clothing, blew muddied photographs and bits of paper rattling past my feet, but I hardly noticed. My head was still full of the sound of Sarah Louise's name. I didn't know what color her hair was, if her eyes were blue, or brown, or green, but I knew I'd carry her voice with me the rest of my days.

Debris-filled pools dotted streets, even though the gulf had retreated, and a thick layer of foul-smelling slime coated everything. Horses and cattle strayed into yards and wandered up to everyone they encountered, eager to find their owners. I didn't see a blade of grass for them, but I was soon searching for it, just as they must have, longing for a glimpse of green, just one wisp of something fresh in the air.

We passed two dead boys in an alley, twins about five years old, still holding on to each other. I stared at their small bodies, not willing to leave them, hoping my own family wasn't lying like this somewhere, too. Josiah found a busted shovel nearby and offered to help me bury them.

It was what I wanted, and what I would've wanted someone to do for those I loved as well, but I shook my head. "How will their mother ever know what happened if we bury them?"

Josiah started digging. "She ain't alive or she woulda already been 'round."

I blinked and stood aside.

While Josiah dug a shallow grave and buried them, I scratched the words, "Twin boys, age 5," on a board and drove it into the ground with the back of the shovel. I was finally able to turn my back on them, but on the next corner we found another body, a woman this time.

A man sat near her on the curb with a bottle of whiskey in his hands. I asked if he knew who she was, and he shook his head.

"I've been looking for my wife all day, but that ain't her."

He sipped at the bottle but didn't appear drunk. I waited to hear more, and just when I figured he'd said all he wanted, he added, "I couldn't get home last night and now everything is gone, just washed away."

I tried to get him to go on, but he refused, saying he wanted to help us lay her away. He used a board to pull back the wet sand Josiah shoveled, all the while mumbling a name—his wife's, I reckoned.

When we'd dug the hole large enough, he helped me lay her in the grave with such tenderness, it near made my heart break in two. I found a corrugated washboard to place over her face and refilled the grave. We stood over her a moment, quiet, then the man thanked me and turned south toward the gulf.

Up ahead, gangs of men loaded bodies onto mule-drawn drays that only yesterday had hauled groceries or grain or beer, and on every street corner we saw people, cut and bruised, clothes in shreds, asking about missing children, husbands, wives.

We passed a mule impaled on an iron fence, a cow bawling from the top of a shed, and a man dressed in a nun's habit. He said the sisters at the Ursuline convent had pulled his bruised and naked body through a window, saving his life, and had given him the only clothes they had.

Another man who had lost his wife and four children claimed he'd been swept into the gulf where he floated all night hanging onto a steamer trunk before being washed miraculously back to shore. And soon after, we came across a lisping boy, no more than eight, who told without a single tear how he'd watched his mother die.

Stories crowded the streets, and through all these tales and others, I saw not a trace of emotion. Eyes stared, glazed and without light. Hearts appeared numb. The panic and loss that had gripped us all seemed to have been replaced with a bewildered calm.

Doors swung open to the houses that had withstood the storm, and anyone, rich or poor, white or colored, merchant or servant, was welcomed and fed. A woman who'd been carrying water to the men working in her street offered me a ladle and didn't hesitate to let Josiah drink, too. We had our fill, gulping greedily, almost emptying the bucket.

By the time we finally turned onto what was left of Thirty-fifth Street, I figured we must've been walking for at least six hours, maybe more.

Right away I saw that Ella Rose's house had been swept away, as were most homes along that side of the street. Ezra and Josiah's place was gone, too; only pilings marked what once had been. But most of Uncle Nate's house still stood. Even the big ash tree sat anchored in the front yard with its stark limbs stretching skyward for leaves long gone.

As we neared the house, I could see more. The barn

out back was gone, and there was no sign of Archer or Deuce, Uncle Nate's horses. The dray or buggy, either. The neighbor's house on the south side had been swept up against the wall, leaving a mangled pile of lumber as high as Andy and Will's bedroom windows. In this case, it may have protected the house. Only a portion of my uncle's roof and veranda appeared damaged. The front stairs had been swept away, but the north stairs, which led to the kitchen door at the side of the house, had remained intact. Oddly, the screen was still attached.

Gratitude swelled inside me. The house looked far better than many. Surely everyone was safe inside.

Josiah grinned when he saw Ezra clearing debris from the kitchen stairs. "My granddaddy look fine," he said.

I nodded and smiled back at him. "I bet he'll be surprised to see you."

We moved as fast as we could, helping each other over the splintered roofs and broken furniture that stood between us and Ezra, but there was no sneaking up on the man. He heard us coming, and when he saw Josiah, he dropped his armful of litter and laughed out loud.

I stood back a moment, watching Ezra and Josiah hug and laugh and hug again, then I bolted up the steps, forgetting all about my aches and pains, lost in one thought, one wish.

I burst through the screen door and saw Aunt Julia scooping mud from the kitchen floor and scraping it into a bucket. She just stood there for a moment, mouth open, blinking at me.

"Oh, sweet Jesus," she whispered. The muddied dustpan hit the floor, and she threw her arms around me. "We thought you were dead."

She turned me loose and cradled Josiah's face in her hands. "Thank God you're both safe." She pulled us through the dining room, toward the parlor, hollering all the way. "Everyone, come see! Come see who's here!"

We picked our way across the muddy warped floor, and before we got to the parlor, Andy and Will let out a whoop. "It's Seth and Josiah!" they yelled. I heard feet on the stairs, and seconds later Matt and Lucas had me in such a tight hold I could hardly breathe.

"Mama, Papa," I gasped between squeezes, "Ella Rose—are they okay?"

"Sure, they're all okay," Matt said, grinning.

Then Mama was there, wrapping her arms around me, covering me with kisses, leaving my cheeks wet with her tears.

"Where's Papa?" I asked.

She hesitated, then smiled up at me. "We expect him soon."

She'd said it with conviction, but I'd caught the

moment of uncertainty. I'd seen the shadow in her eyes.

I glanced at the broken windows, the shredded curtains, the muddied carpet and furniture. I saw the hole they'd chopped in the floor to let in the rising water so the house wouldn't float away.

But I didn't see Kate.

I jerked back around to Mama and noticed for the first time that her eyes were red and swollen. Aunt Julia's were, too. My heart splintered, and I swore I could hear it breaking apart, just like the crunching of houses I'd heard during the crystal lulls last night. I remembered the child on the beach, the sand on her lashes and cheeks. I saw the mangled snake of debris, heard Sarah Louise Ellison's faint calls all over again, and the room swam. Mama called my name, but I couldn't answer.

She slid her hand over my forehead. "I bet you boys haven't eaten a thing these past two days."

"No, ma'am," Josiah said. "There weren't much to be had."

In Josiah's apologetic tone, I glimpsed just how much he'd been watching out for me since we'd left work yesterday. I pushed Mama's hand away. I couldn't think about that now. "I'm okay, Mama. Just tell me about Kate."

"Kate?" She gave me a puzzled look, then sighed with understanding. "Oh, Seth, you needn't have worried. She's asleep upstairs. Ella Rose is up there, too, looking after Elliott for your Aunt Julia."

I closed my eyes and let her words settle inside me. They were all safe. But when I glanced at Aunt Julia, I knew there was more.

"What else?" I asked, looking from face to face. "Where's Uncle Nate? And Ben?"

Aunt Julia's eyes filled with tears, and Mama pulled in a deep breath. "Your papa has been out looking for them all day," she said, "for Mr. Covington, too. None of them made it home last night."

I remembered the flying slate, the rushing water, and I put my arms around Aunt Julia. "Josiah and I made it back," I whispered. "They will, too. We'll head out right now and help look for them."

Josiah nodded, but Aunt Julia gave us a grateful glance and said no.

"The streets will soon be far too dark and dangerous."

"That's true," Mama said. "Besides, you boys have to rest and eat something. Hopefully, your papa will come home soon with good news."

"And if not," Aunt Julia said, "maybe you can look for them in the morning?"

I hugged her again. "We'll go at first light." I glanced toward the stairs. "How is Ella Rose?"

"Frightened," Mama said. "There has been no word of her father. None from her uncle and his family, either, but she's a strong girl and a true blessing. We haven't had to worry once about the care of the children." She patted my hand and smiled. "You go on up and see for yourself while I fix us some supper. Nothing special," she warned, "but it'll be filling."

I nodded, and headed upstairs. Mud coated the treads all the way to the landing, and when I opened the door to Ben's bedroom, I saw a gaping hole in the roof. The room had been soaked, plaster and splintered lumber lay everywhere, and the mattress had been leaned against the wall to dry out.

I opened the door next to Ben's and found Kate asleep on the bed. I leaned close to her, pushed damp curls from her pink cheeks, and her eyelids fluttered open. When she realized who I was, she giggled and wrapped her arms around my neck. My heart ached with gratitude.

We walked hand in hand to the next room, and I knocked softly on the door. Ella Rose pulled it open and stood there, staring at me. Without a single word, she moved into my arms and rested her cheek against my chest.

"I knew you'd come," she whispered.

Chapter

17

Mama asked a hundred questions while she cleaned our wounds and smeared salve over our cuts. Everyone wanted to know how we'd survived, how our neighbors had fared, if our house was still standing, but it seemed impossible to put all we'd seen into words. Josiah shot me a helpless glance, and with a shake of his head, sat there speechless. I struggled to tell it all as best I could, but even the sparest words put me back in the midst of wind, water, and lifeless eyes. When I'd finally spoken the last of it, we all sat in dead silence.

Kate looked at the bent heads, the prayerful hands folded in laps, and said, "A-a-a-men."

Everyone laughed and wiped away tears. I laughed, too, relieved to be shed of the dark memories for the moment and back safe again in Aunt Julia's parlor.

All day Sunday, odors had intensified under the hot sun. The stench made it difficult to even think of eating supper, but I crowded around the freshly scrubbed dining table with everyone else, grateful to be there.

We sat on whatever we could find that had been scraped clean of mud. Lucas squeezed between me and Matt, holding a wounded cat he'd found this morning. He'd set her broken leg, and she lay secure in his lap, splint and all, till Mama fussed and made him put her down.

Kate hadn't left my side since she woke up. She reached for my hand under the table, wrapped her fingers around my thumb, and once again I felt my breath catch in my throat.

Mama put steaming bowls of grits in front of us, then surprised me by asking that I give the blessing, something only Papa did. I looked at the faces circled around the table, thinking about how often I'd wanted Mama and Papa to see me as a man. Now I was being called upon to step into Papa's shoes, but it was nothing like I'd imagined.

Mama glanced at me, waiting, so I lowered my head and searched for the right words.

"Our Father," I said. "For the lives that were spared, for the homes left standing, and for the food set before us, we are truly grateful."

Children strung like pearls, brown fingers grasping baseballs.

"We ask your blessings for the many that were lost last night . . ."

My name is Sarah Louise Ellison.

". . . for the many who are wounded or alone . . ."

Empty, stunned faces.

". . . and for all the lonely loved ones left behind."

I peered up at Aunt Julia and Ella Rose. "We also ask that You watch over Uncle Nate, Ben, and Mr. Covington, and help Papa bring them home safe to us."

Aunt Julia looked up at me, eyes soft with gratitude, but like Josiah, I felt something in my bones, something dark and heavy. I opened my mouth, but no more words would come.

"A-a-a-men," Kate said, once again bringing smiles to the strained faces around the table.

Everyone picked up their spoons while I stared at the puddle of pale golden butter on top of my grits. Then with the suddenness of a cat pouncing on its prey, hunger hit.

I quickly emptied my bowl, sure I'd never eaten anything that tasted so good, and when I looked up again, Mama was standing over me, dipping her big spoon back into the pot.

"I reckon it might take every bit of this to make up for two days of doing without."

Mama filled my bowl again, then Josiah's, and set the pot on the table.

"If it hadn't been for Ezra," Aunt Julia said, "we'd all be going hungry tonight. He managed to get a lot of the food up to the attic before the water rose."

"Good thing he didn't put it over Ben's room," Lucas said, "or the fish would've been eating it tonight instead of us."

Ezra laughed, and for the first time, I realized how much he sounded like Josiah.

By the time we'd finished eating, the light had faded, and Ezra lit candles for the kitchen and parlor. While he helped the boys wash up supper dishes, Ella Rose played with Kate and Elliott. Mama wanted to go back to scraping up mud, but Aunt Julia wouldn't hear of it.

"You've been working hard all day, Eliza. There'll be plenty of time tomorrow for dealing with this mud." She pulled two chairs to the window and made Mama sit with her to watch for Papa.

Later Matt sat next to me in the parlor on a warped bench. He was quiet, and I was content to have it so. Knowing he was safe beside me was enough, but after a while, he turned toward a south window and whispered, "I saw it coming."

There was no need to ask what he saw. I knew he was talking about the gulf.

"I saw it rise up, Seth—must've been near twenty feet high—and rush toward us, scraping up everything in its path. I even saw a horse on the crest, spinning wild, over and over. I was afraid it was Archer or Deuce." He sucked in a breath. "I thought we were dead for sure, Seth, and I didn't hold out much hope for you, either."

I nodded. "Did you find the horses?"

"No, but we found a dead colt on the kitchen stairs and a man tangled in the limbs of the ash tree out front."

"Was he dead, too?"

"Yeah, but not from drowning. The tree was full of snakes, and the man was covered with bites."

"Did Ezra take care of him?"

Matt nodded. "Along with the help of a neighbor behind us on Broadway. Mr. Hodges's horse and wagon made it through the storm okay, so he came 'round to pick up the dead. I wanted to help, too, but Mama wouldn't let me out of the house. I saw through the window, though." He looked up at me, eyes wide. "Mr. Hodges must've had at least thirty bodies on that wagon, Seth, and all of them were friends and neighbors of Aunt Julia's and Ella Rose's."

I stared at him while the reality of what he'd said sunk in. They'd lost far more than I'd realized. I glanced at the younger boys sitting on the floor, wondering if they'd seen, too. Matt leaned close and whispered, "Don't worry; I didn't let them near the windows."

"It's Thomas!" Mama called.

I picked up Elliott, and we all crowded into the kitchen to see who Papa was bringing home, but only one set of footsteps sounded on the staircase. Papa, haggard and dirty, stepped into the doorway and blinked in the candlelight. When his eyes rested on me and Josiah, relief flooded his face, and for a moment, I thought I saw tears. But with one glance at Ella Rose, his joy disappeared. He reached for her hands.

"You found my daddy?" Her voice sounded small and fragile.

He gave her a slow but definite nod, and, as if she'd known all along, she said, "He's dead, isn't he?"

Papa nodded again. "He was at the Ritter Café when the printing presses on the second floor fell through. I found him in the temporary morgue set up at the wharf and buried him myself. When things are better, I'll show you where." He pulled a small handkerchief-wrapped bundle from his pocket and placed it in her hand. "I thought you might want these."

Ella Rose unfolded the handkerchief. A pocket watch, two rings, and a gold rose tiepin lay in the white cloth. She fingered the smaller ring. "My mama's wedding band," she whispered. "Daddy put it on his little finger when she died last year and never took it off."

"What about her cousin?" Mama asked. "Henry, and his family?"

Papa shook his head. "Their house is gone. I asked everywhere I went, but there's been no news."

"Nothing of Mr. Farrell, either?" I asked. "Or Zach Judson and his family?"

Again he shook his head. "Nothing."

Ella Rose stared over Papa's shoulder for a long moment, then stuffed the bundle into her apron pocket and wrapped her arms around him. "Thank you, Mr. Braeden, for taking such good care of my daddy." She kissed him on the cheek, and when she turned to take Elliott from my arms, I saw a glint of something hard in her eyes.

I stared at her, surprised. She rested Elliott on her hip and waited with us to hear the rest of the news.

Aunt Julia hadn't said a word, but her face held little hope. When Papa turned to her, his eyes were full of pain and regret.

"I'm sorry, Julia." He pulled in a ragged breath. "I looked everywhere for them."

Mama sent Lucas for water while Papa slumped into a chair and leaned over the table, his face in his hands.

Aunt Julia kneeled beside him. "We all know how hard you tried, Thomas. No one could've done more." She glanced up at me. "But there *have* been blessings in this house. Seth was spared, and Josiah was, too. We have a lot to be thankful for." She patted Papa's hand. "Maybe tomorrow," she said, and with slow, measured movements, she removed her apron, folded it, and went upstairs.

Andy and Will watched her go, eyes dry but full of pain. When they headed for the stairs outside, I nudged Matt and Lucas. They nodded and took off after them, which made me feel somewhat better. At least they wouldn't be alone in the dark.

I left Papa in Mama's care, grabbed Kate, and followed Ella Rose to the parlor. She sat on the bench, shifted Elliott to her shoulder, and with a rocking motion, began singing softly to him.

I didn't know what to do. What could be done for someone who'd lost a father, a home, friends, everything that was dear to her? We hadn't heard a word of Henry and his family, either, so there was a good chance that Ella Rose was truly alone in this world.

I slipped onto the bench beside her, feeling helpless in my need to comfort her. All I could say was "I'm sorry."

She continued to rock and sing, never once pausing in her lullaby.

Later, Aunt Julia came back downstairs. I searched her face, wondering if she'd been alone up there in the dark with her sorrow, but I was surprised to see no sign of grieving. She carried a large stack of clean clothes, and in it, I recognized Ben's blue work shirt and Uncle Nate's pants.

"I'll share my room with Eliza, Ella Rose, and the little ones." She handed a comforter to Ezra. "You and Josiah can sleep on the clean table if you like, and the rest of you will have to make do with Andy and Will's room till Ben's roof is fixed."

It seemed to be the best solution, but it was the first time I'd ever known Mama and Papa to sleep in separate bedrooms.

"Ezra," Aunt Julia continued, "would you and Josiah kindly move Will's bed into my room for Ella Rose and Kate?"

"Yes'm," Ezra said, and the two of them headed upstairs.

It seemed odd to think that only yesterday we'd had our own house, our own beds and clothing. Now we had nothing we could call our own. I glanced at Ella Rose. It was far worse for her.

I pulled some clothes from the stack and went to the kitchen to wash up a bit. The city water lines were down and clean water was scarce. Ezra had been hauling it from the Hodges' indoor cistern more than a block away, so I was careful not to use too much. I wet a rag, cleaned up as best I could, and dressed in Ben's clothes. One look at my old tattered shirt and pants and I knew they could never be repaired. I pulled my barlow knife from the dirty pocket and with it came a handful of tiny brown petals.

Kate's funeral flowers. I'd stuffed them into my pocket yesterday at the rental, along with the baseball.

I stared at them. Only two nights ago the sweet smell of jasmine had lulled me to sleep.

I blew out the putrid stench that pervaded every breath, cupped the shriveled brown petals in my hands, and brought them to my nose. A faint scent still clung to them, and I breathed in the fragile sweetness.

It smelled like life.

I pulled open Ben's clean pocket and carefully poured the brown petals inside.

Chapter
~ 18 ~

When I woke Monday morning, Papa was already up. I left the boys sleeping on their pallets, eased down the stairs, and found him in the kitchen with Ezra and Josiah, sitting around a breakfast of soda crackers and water.

"It'll be daybreak soon," Papa said. "Better eat something."

He slid the tin of crackers to me, and I nodded. "I'll be ready to go when you are."

"Yessir. Me too, sir," Josiah said.

"Do you have a plan?" I asked.

"Ezra will stay," Papa said. "He'll rebuild the outhouse and help the boys gather all the lumber, slate, and nails they can to repair the roof and veranda. With the wagon bridge gone and the three railroad bridges wiped out, it'll be a while before new supplies can be shipped in."

"What about us?" I asked.

"We'll travel each road between home and Nate's lumberyard, then check the hospitals and morgues."

"Do you think there's still a chance we can find them alive?"

Papa looked up at me, then closed his eyes to my question. "I heard talk last night about a call for burial at sea," he said. "The temporary morgues filled quickly yesterday. Identifying and burying all the bodies seems nigh impossible now."

I nodded, thinking of Aunt Julia and Ella Rose, about how they'd feel if the worst should come to pass. There'd be no flowers, no good-byes, no final resting place for their loved ones.

"Then we'll have to find them soon," I said. "What about food and water for the island?"

"The water mains are down and the outdoor cisterns are salty, so there's not much to be had. The provisions left in markets and warehouses will be rationed. A few men left yesterday on a twenty-foot launch for the mainland, trying to get help." He glanced up at Josiah. "Did Ezra talk to you about being watchful?"

Josiah nodded. "Yessir."

"Watchful of what?" I asked.

"There's been some looting. A few colored men were shot yesterday."

"Shot?" I glanced at Josiah, and he quickly looked away. "What'd they steal that was worth killing them over?"

"Rings. They were cutting fingers off dead bodies to get to the rings."

I stared at Papa, my skin crawling at the thought. "You think Josiah might be in danger?"

"Not if he's careful about the way he checks the dead. You, too, Seth. Just be mindful, both of you."

I nodded, but remembering all the bodies we came across yesterday, it seemed impossible that anyone could suffer something as repulsive as cutting off a swollen finger.

Papa slid his chair back and stood up. "We'd best be going."

I nodded and followed him down the stairs into the already steamy dawn. Once on the littered ground, Josiah glanced back at his grandfather and waved. Even in the half-light I could see the hesitancy in Ezra's farewell, the uncertainty about his grandson's safety. I stole a quick look at Papa, and though I saw many things, fear for his son was not one of them.

We headed east, picking our way over every conceivable sort of wreckage. The brutal stench grew, rising with the sun, till we felt forced to tie our handkerchiefs across our noses and mouths. It gave little relief other than to let us feel as if we'd done something, no matter how small, to put a barrier between ourselves and the putrid odors.

For hours we combed the streets that lay between the lumberyard and home, searching for Ben and Uncle Nate, but without success.

We saw a man on horseback—Major Fayling, Josiah said—issuing orders to a group of ragged artillerymen and local militia. He told them to press into service every able-bodied man they could find to help haul away the corpses. We ducked behind an overturned house, determined to stick to our mission, but I could see the guilt in Papa's face. He would've helped them right then if he could've.

When the men were gone, we continued on, asking questions of everyone we could, checking bodies as we went. My stomach reeled to the brink of upheaval every time I gazed into another swollen, distorted face, making me wonder if we could possibly recognize our own people should we happen upon them.

As the morning disappeared, I began to think we had no chance of finding them, especially when we saw what was left of the lumberyard. It was gone, wiped clean, as if the store and all the stacked lumber had never existed.

Papa stared at the empty space till I took his arm and led him away. "We need to get on to the hospitals and morgues," I said.

He nodded, and we made our way farther east.

I tried to keep my thoughts centered on the job ahead of us and avoided looking at the twenty-foot ridge of debris looming to the south. I didn't want to see the bright flash of sunlight from the shard of mirror. I didn't want to feel the pain that brought me to my knees yesterday. Instead I concentrated on the path ahead and on bringing Aunt Julia news that she could live with.

Everywhere we looked, we saw men and wagons crawling through the fly-infested city, picking up bodies. We managed to skirt the dead gangs and were happy to find that the hospitals had weathered the storm well enough. We hurried through wards, searching rows of wounded, asking questions of nurses and attendants, but there was no sign of Ben and Uncle Nate. Papa looked drained and miserable. John Sealy Hospital had been our last real hope of finding them alive.

Back outside, we headed west again, toward one of the temporary morgues set up north of the Strand. It soon became clear that passage through the business district would be almost impossible. Fallen telephone poles, tangled wires, and dead horses crowded the streets. Piles of bricks, wrecked wagons, and tons of rotting vegetables lay everywhere.

We spent precious time picking our way past it all, but once there, I got my first close and staggering glimpse of the rail yards and harbor. I saw hundreds of boxcars tumbled this way and that, their valuable loads of flour, grain, and cotton ruined. And from one end of the wharf to the other, sailboats and tugs lay sunk or in jumbled confusion. But it was the sight of all those bodies bobbing in the water that left me breathless and sick. Men with long hooks pulled them into boats, as they must've done all day long, and I couldn't help but wonder how many hundreds more must be scattered across Galveston Bay. We turned our backs on the battered harbor, and Papa led us to the makeshift morgue set up near the docks.

A blazing afternoon sun beat down on the crumpled metal roof, turning the vast shed into an oven. Bluebottle flies droned, and the smell almost buckled my knees.

I couldn't move.

Rows and rows of dead stretched into the recesses of the great building. Hundreds of men, women, and children lay in the heat, some covered, some exposed. White and colored, Chinese and Mexicans—every nationality you might imagine.

Survivors of the storm moved silently between the rows, their faces furrowed in a bewildered mix of hope and fear and horror. They lifted coverings, searching for something familiar in the swollen faces, and occasionally I'd hear the dreadful, choking sobs of recognition.

I braced myself for the task ahead, but as Papa had feared, the decision to dispose of the bodies at sea must've already been made that morning. A troop of men, white and colored alike, were driven into the shed by bayonet to assist in the work of loading the dead on barges tied up near the morgue.

We'd almost arrived too late.

While we hurriedly searched for anything recognizable among the bodies, the men began their grisly work. I worried that we might be forced at gunpoint to join them, but the guards stood firm in their immediate job and never looked our way. They carried kegs of whiskey and freely passed tin cups to workers, but even with that strong fortification, I saw man after man stand aside to steady their stomachs. My heart went out to them, as well as my thanks to God that I didn't have to face their terrible assignment.

We managed to stay ahead of the workers in our search, but in the end, we had to leave empty-handed. I was almost glad. The thought of Ben and Uncle Nate lying there amidst so much putrefaction was unbearable.

Gratefully, I hurried out with Josiah and found Papa clasping the hand of a big man wearing clothes far too small for him.

"I'm ready for the next flood," he said, pointing to his legs.

Papa smiled at the absurdity of seeing this huge man in pants that struck midcalf, then turned to more serious topics.

His friend confirmed that the decision to load the dead on barges for burial at sea had indeed been made that morning, and already the first barge was almost full. There would be no need to check the other morgues.

"They're saying that if the bodies aren't moved by sundown, they'll have to take them out in pieces tomorrow. So they're barging them eighteen miles out, weighting them down with scrap metal, and giving them to the sea."

Papa nodded, but the same shadow of guilt I'd seen earlier darkened his face again.

"I'm on my way to the rail yard," the man said. "A whole trainload of supplies was just turned back 'cause the bridge is out. Can you imagine that? All those supplies just sittin' there, and we can't get to 'em. I figure the quicker we get that bridge rebuilt, the quicker I'll get out of these blasted pants and get some real food in me."

Papa smiled, but something had shifted in his face. He discussed the project a bit more while I listened and waited, but I'd already suspected what was coming.

"Can you two make it home without getting into trouble?" he asked.

"Yessir," I said, "but—"

"Good."

Determination glinted in his eyes, just like the day he'd decided to move us all to Galveston. There'd be no talking him out of this.

He squinted against the sun and pointed toward the washed-out railroad bridge. "I'll probably be sleeping in one of those wrecked train cars. I'll need food and water and a change of clothes." He kicked a broken bottle with the toe of his shoe, thinking, then looked back at me. "Matt can do it. He can sleep in the train car with me nights, be home first thing every morning, and get back here again before nightfall with my meals each day. You help him find me this evening, but give yourself enough time to get home before dark."

I nodded, my thoughts skittering from Mama and Aunt Julia to all that needed done at home. I guess he saw the questions in my face because he rested a hand on my shoulder and said, "I have to do this, Seth. You understand, don't you?"

I nodded again, but I didn't understand at all. Mama and Aunt Julia needed him. *I* needed him. Who would tell Aunt Julia that her husband and son hadn't been found, that their bodies would most likely be cast into the sea without tears, without Scripture, without prayers? Who would make sure the family had food and clean water? Who would rebuild the house?

"Your mother was right," Papa said. "There's a reason for everything. Tell her that for me."

I couldn't believe what I was hearing. Anger flashed lightning-hot through me, and this time, I didn't bother hiding it. "What are you saying?" I spit at him. "That your reason for being here right now is to work on a bridge? What about your family?"

He stared at me, and for a brief moment I saw something raw in his face, like a dozen fears had hit him all at once. I watched him draw a shaky breath, and a flush of satisfaction swept over me. Maybe now he finally understood that he couldn't possibly leave us, not at a time like this. But then his jaw clenched and his eyes hardened.

"I need to do this," he said. "We both need to look to what we do best." With a quick turn, he hurried after his friend, then paused to holler over his shoulder. "Bring blankets when you come tonight."

He left me standing in the rubble, never once looking back, never once considering anyone but himself. I glared after him, watching till he disappeared behind a fallen roof, too stunned to think about what to do next.

Josiah glanced over his shoulder at all the men carrying their ghastly burdens to the barge. "Best we get on home, now," he whispered, " 'fore somethin' bad happens."

I glimpsed more bayonets and nodded.

We turned south, headed toward Broadway where there seemed to be less debris, and right away Josiah's long legs put half a block between us. Just as I was about to holler at him to slow down for me, I heard a loud shout.

In seconds, Josiah was surrounded by three bayonets. I ducked behind an overturned buggy, fear thumping wild in my chest, and peered around a busted wheel. He glanced at me, eyes wide, then quickly turned away so the men wouldn't find me.

Josiah was led to a larger group of workers, and it was then I realized why he'd drawn attention. He was lean, but his height made him look as old as any of them. Without another glance in my direction, he fell into step, marching back the way we'd come, north toward the barges. I held my breath while they passed just yards away from me and heard one of the newly pressed workers pleading to be let go.

"For heaven's sake," he said, "don't make me do that. I won't go! You can shoot me if you want to, but I will not and I cannot do what you ask."

The guardsman stopped and called his men to attention. "Load with ball cartridge," he ordered. "Take aim!"

The threat was all the poor man needed. He threw up his hands, and when the guns had been lowered, he hung his head and marched off behind Josiah to the barges.

Even after the footsteps faded, I couldn't move. Flies droned, and overhead, seagulls called and buzzards circled.

I finally slunk away, avoiding the main streets, ducking and hiding all the way home. I could hardly let myself think about what Josiah would be facing. Guilt and horror squirmed inside me, but I knew I couldn't help him. I had to get home.

I had to do what Papa wouldn't.

Chapter

~ 19 ~

Mama must've seen me walking back alone. She ran to meet me at the foot of the stairs, but before I could reach her, Aunt Julia and the four boys raced down, too. Ella Rose stood on the landing near the screen door with Elliott on her hip, holding Kate's hand, waiting like everyone else to hear why I was alone. Elliott's heat-flushed cheek brushed against hers and his chubby fingers tangled in her hair. I stared at her, wishing I didn't have to say anything to anyone, wishing I could forget what had happened and just go to her.

But I couldn't. Papa had seen to that.

Everyone gathered around, but I waited till I saw Ezra step from behind the corner of the raised basement before I began.

"What happened?" Mama asked. "Where's your papa?" Her voice sounded fearful, breathy with impatience.

"He's okay," I reassured her. "He was needed to help

rebuild the railroad bridge. I'm to show Matt where to take his meals this evening."

She let out a relieved sigh, but her eyes quickly glazed over as she considered what this would mean to us.

"How long will he be away?"

I shrugged. "He didn't say. He just said to tell you that you were right about there being a reason for everything."

I hadn't bothered to keep the sarcasm out of my voice. I thought for sure Mama would be as mad as I was that Papa had left us at a time like this, but instead, I saw a slow smile curl the corners of her lips. When she kissed me on the cheek, I felt I must've missed something, but I didn't have time to think about it. Aunt Julia had already turned her pale, freckled face to mine, and I couldn't ignore what had to be said.

"Any news for us?" she asked.

Her voice sounded small and brittle, stripped of hope, and my heart near broke just hearing it. I wrapped my arms around her, wishing I could find the words to lessen her misery, but all I could say was "I'm sorry, Aunt Julia."

She hugged me tight, and over her shoulder, I saw Andy and Will hang their heads. "I'll try again in the morning," I told her. "First thing."

She shook her head. "No more searching, Seth. No

more." Then, as if there were more important things to consider, she said, "You must be so tired and thirsty. Let me get you some water."

Andy piped up, quick to volunteer. "I'll get it for him, Mama."

She shook her head, patted him on the shoulder, and headed for the stairs. I was relieved to see Ella Rose follow her inside.

Andy's eyes welled with tears, and Will swiped at his wet cheeks with the back of his sleeve. Ezra still stood at the corner of the raised basement, waiting. I didn't know how to tell him about Josiah. It wasn't fair that he'd been taken and I'd been spared, but I was finally coming to understand that there had been little in Josiah and Ezra's world that had ever been fair.

He, Mama, and the boys listened quietly while I told about all I'd seen, and when I was through, Mama couldn't hold back her tears any longer.

"What were they thinking? He's just sixteen." She wiped her eyes with the tail of her apron and looked up at Ezra. "I'm so sorry," she whispered. "We'll keep Josiah in our prayers."

"Thank you, ma'am," he said softly. "But he's a powerful strong boy. I 'spect we be seeing him when the work be done."

He thanked me, too, and went back to building the outhouse, leaving me to marvel at the way he accepted what he couldn't change. I hadn't handled things nearly so well.

"Come on, Andy," Matt said. "Let's go pry those nails loose like Ezra asked."

Lucas nodded. "Yeah, he has a surprise for us when we finish, remember?"

Andy shook his head. "Maybe in a little while."

Will sat on the shady bottom step, still sniffling. Mama squeezed around him, headed back to the kitchen, but not before she gave him a kiss on the top of his head.

Matt and Lucas glanced at me, not sure what to do. I wasn't either, but since Papa had abandoned us, I figured it was up to me to do something. And soon.

I heard Ezra hammering on the outhouse and headed around back. He'd already filled in the old hole, dug a fresh one, and managed to get the new building almost finished, but it was Aunt Julia and the boys I wanted to talk to him about most. I wasn't sure what Papa would've done if he'd been here, or if he even knew how to deal with a loss as great as theirs, but I had to start somewhere.

Ezra saw me coming, pulled a rag from his back pocket, and wiped his face.

"It's looking real good, Ezra."

"Yessir," he said, "it be coming along."

I nodded. "I was just wondering if you could tell me how my aunt is doing?"

He shook his head. "Grieving. But the missus, she be burying it deeper than that gulf out there."

I wasn't sure what I could do about that, but it seemed that she and Ella Rose had been spending more time together. Maybe they'd found a way to share each other's pain in a way that none of us could. At least I hoped so. "And how about Andy and Will?"

"Aw, they's good boys, and strong, too. They's a big comfort to their mama, even if she don't see it yet."

I nodded, thankful that Ezra was watching out for them. He showed me the big pile of lumber and slate that he and the boys had gathered this morning, enough to repair the veranda and the roof over Ben's room. I pointed to a smaller stack of odd-length boards beside it. "What are those for?"

Ezra laughed, making me think of Josiah again.

"Why, that there lumber is gonna hep make a new treehouse for all them boys," he said.

The storm had ripped the old tree fort from the ash in the front yard and washed it away. Building another must be the surprise Lucas spoke of.

I smiled. "Good idea, Ezra."

"Busy hands can sometimes hep heal lonesome hearts," he said.

He turned back to his work, and I found myself staring at my own hands. Everyone would be looking to me now.

Nearby, Matt and Lucas had begun pulling nails, but Andy and Will still hadn't joined them. I didn't know what I could say to make things easier for those two boys, but I needed to try. I turned to find them, but they found me first.

"Seth," Andy said, "me and Will have been wondering about Papa and Ben. Would you tell us what you think happened? Mama won't talk about it at all."

Their question almost knocked the wind out of me, like the time I was eight and fell off Papa's horse. I hit the ground so hard I was afraid I'd never draw another breath.

The thought of telling them what I suspected fluttered sick inside me, but if it were me in their place, I couldn't have rested easy, either, till I knew something, no matter how small. I braced myself for what needed done. "I will," I said to them and led them back to the steps.

They settled near my feet while I grappled with the words tumbling in my head. "I suppose," I said, "we should begin with what we know."

They nodded, faces grim but expectant.

"Your papa spoke to your mama by telephone early Saturday, the day of the storm, and he told her that he and Ben were securing the lumberyard as best they could. They must've worked really hard trying to save the business, but I figure they might've stayed too long."

The boys' eyes, still red, never left my face.

"You see," I continued, "when Josiah and I made it back here that afternoon, the streets were already flooded. We struck out again, right away, for the rental, and before we were even halfway there, we saw people get hit by flying bricks and slate and knocked over by all kinds of debris sweeping down the streets. Many of them were pulled under and didn't come back up."

"So you think they drowned?" Andy asked.

"I think it's possible."

"But you didn't find their bodies, did you?"

"No, and we looked really hard."

"Then maybe they got saved," Will said. "Maybe they're sitting in someone's house right now, hurt, and they can't get home just yet."

I nodded. "Maybe. That's why we won't give up."

The boys sat quiet for a moment, then Andy blew out a long breath. "Thanks, Seth."

"Yeah," Will said. "Thanks."

I watched them walk around back to pull nails with Matt and Lucas, and when I rose from the step, I glimpsed Aunt Julia standing just inside the screen door, my cup of water in her hand.

That evening I led Matt through the back streets to the rail yard, watching carefully for anyone who might take me from his side. I wished I could protect him from seeing the wagons loaded with dead, the dazed, half-naked people looking for loved ones, but it was impossible. I feared what it must be doing to him. As much as I'd seen, my stomach still knotted at the sight of each bloated body; my heart still ached when I looked into all those desperate, searching faces. Matt never spoke a word about it the whole way, but I understood why. There just weren't words big enough to speak of such things.

We found Papa near the old bridge pilings with a half dozen other men, sorting and stacking storm-wrecked timbers. It looked like it might take a while to gather all that was needed before the real work could begin. His clothes were soaked and his eyes red, blood-shot from salty sweat, but he smiled when he saw us.

Matt set his basket of food and clothing down next to the water jugs I'd carried and went off to prowl around the stacks of timber. Papa dropped to the ground close by, breathing hard from his work. "Glad to see you made it safe," he said. "I've already seen too many boys your age pressed into service, forced to clear debris and such."

"I'm fine," I told him, "but Josiah was taken to the barges right after you left us."

Papa cringed, and grief welled in his eyes.

I stared at him, surprised that Josiah's misfortune would bring him pain, and even more surprised that I was finding satisfaction in his misery. But it was all his fault. If he hadn't so willingly shirked his duty to family and home, Josiah might be with his grandfather instead of loading barges with unspeakable cargo and heading to the gulf.

Papa shook his head as if to rid himself of the horror he'd glimpsed. "I heard they don't keep the dead gangs long, Seth. He'll probably be let go tomorrow morning when the barges come back in, but keep in mind that they may come looking for him again." He pulled in a deep breath. "Matt should be okay walking to and from the house," he said, "but if you get stopped on the way home, be sure to tell them you're just sixteen and that you're the only man left in the house. They'll let you go."

"Josiah's sixteen, too," I said, "and they took him anyway."

Papa said nothing, but I knew what he was thinking, I knew what was truly in his heart. He thought Josiah and I were different.

"It's late," Papa said, squinting at the sun. "You'd better get on back or it'll get dark on you."

I nodded, ready to be done with him, but he stopped me.

"Did you tell your mama what I asked?"

I frowned, trying to remember, then it came back to me.

"Sure, Papa," I said, bitterness in every word. "I told

her just what you said, that she was right about there being a reason for everything."

"Good," he muttered. "That's good. Get on back to her then, and I'll see you as soon as I can."

He pushed himself up and went back to his sorting and stacking.

I turned toward home, and by the time I reached Thirty-fifth Street, the sun had disappeared, tempering the jagged wreckage and leaving a halo of pink and purple around bare trees and splintered rooftops. I climbed the stairs, trying not to think about my hard feelings toward Papa, trying to focus on what needed done tomorrow, but I couldn't stop wondering why his message to Mama was so important to him.

Chapter

— 20 —

I woke early Tuesday morning clinging to the edge of my mattress with a knee in my back. During the night, Lucas, Andy, and Will had traded their pallets for Papa's empty side of the bed, and now they lay in a jumbled, sweaty mess from the headboard down. After all they'd endured, though, I couldn't be mad at them.

I eased from the bed, leaving them room to stretch out, and while I gathered my clothes, thoughts of Josiah stabbed at me. I hoped the worst was over for him, that he'd be coming home today, yet seeing him again had begun to worry me some. What he'd had to do on that barge was bound to haunt him. Things like that had a way of tangling a man's insides, changing the way he saw life, and I feared he might never be the same.

The awful stench that had swamped the island hadn't eased, but as I dressed, I finally smelled something else. A faint, warm scent challenged each putrid breeze from the window, drawing me to the kitchen quicker than any call to breakfast.

I hurried downstairs, my stomach already growling, and sat at the kitchen table while Mama tended a big skillet of pan bread. I'd been missing her warm, yeasty loaves, but Aunt Julia's sourdough starter, kept by the sink, had been ruined when the wave swamped the house. Mama explained that it would take a while to produce another good starter, and that till then, we'd have to settle for pan bread and baking-powder biscuits. I wasn't finding it hard to do. I watched, impatient, while she turned the round loaf onto a plate and called Ezra in to eat.

"I found him working by candlelight this morning," she told me, slicing the bread into wedges. "He was scraping dried mud off the floors, and as soon as the sky brightened a bit, he headed off to finish up the outhouse."

I glanced at the scraped floor, still dirty but ready for scrubbing when more water was available. "Aunt Julia is lucky to have him."

Mama nodded. "Especially now."

I reached for a steaming piece of bread. "Did you know he gathered lumber scraps yesterday for another tree fort? He thinks that giving the boys something fun to do will help with Andy and Will's grieving."

Mama smiled. "He's a smart man. He sure deserves

more than his lot in life. Is there any chance that you and Josiah could rebuild his house?"

I stared at her. Just the mention of Josiah's name plunged me back into that morgue. I pushed the grisly images aside, like I'd done a hundred times since yesterday, and thought about what Mama asked.

"I'll add it to my list. Aunt Julia's house has to be repaired before anything else, though."

She nodded and started another batch of bread cooking. "So what's on your list for today?"

"The roof. Gotta get it done before the next rain."

She smiled and pushed a jar of fig preserves across the table to me. "Your papa would be proud. That's exactly what he would do."

I frowned while I spooned sweet preserves onto my bread. Proud or not, since Papa hadn't seen fit to be here, I didn't see why either of us had to give him another thought. I plunked the spoon back into the jar and took a big bite of my bread. "This is real good, Mama," I said, changing the subject. "Oughta keep me fine for a few hours at least."

She raised an eyebrow and shook her head. "You'd better hope our provisions hold out till they get the rails fixed, or we'll all be going hungry for a while."

Ezra came in about the same time I heard footsteps overhead. The boys must've smelled Mama's pan bread, which meant the kitchen would fill up fast. I wolfed down the rest of my breakfast and headed to the pile of scavenged lumber out back, but I wasn't quite ready for work yet. Something had been tugging at my mind ever since I got back Sunday.

I searched the scrap lumber, found a small piece of scuffed mahogany, and pulled out my pocketknife. In rough block letters, I carved SARAH LOUISE ELLISON into the wood. When I finished, I wedged it into the bare branches of the small magnolia tree near the back of the stairs. I had no flowers, but even if I had, it would've still been a sad offering. I remembered Kate's jasmine petals, emptied my pocket into my hand, and brought them to my face. Only the memory of their sweetness remained, but I sprinkled the tiny brown fragments on the ground below the tree anyway and stood back.

"It'll have to do for now, Sarah Louise," I whispered, "but I reckon you and God understand that better than anyone."

I headed for the lumber pile and went to work, sorting and measuring, cutting and nailing. Through the hole in the roof, I heard Ella Rose singing nursery rhymes in the parlor with Kate and Elliott. I'd been seeing something dark in her ever since she'd gotten the news about her father, but now, hearing the happiness in her voice made me think that maybe I'd imagined it. I listened, hardly moving, till Mama and Aunt Julia disturbed her, saying it was time to get some more mud out of the house.

The parlor and dining-room carpets had been ruined. So had the sofa and Uncle Nate's favorite chair. Matt got home in time to help the boys haul them out of the house, but not before Mama had looked him over good. I knew she'd been worried about letting him travel across town alone. When she was satisfied that he was okay, I heard her ask him about Papa. Matt didn't have much to say, only that the men were working twelve-hour shifts around the clock and that rebuilding the bridge might take a while. I'd already accepted that fact, and I was coming to realize I didn't mind being without Papa at all. I could handle what needed doing around here just fine.

Later that morning, I looked up to see Ella Rose across the street with a stick in her hand, standing in the middle of the lot where her house had been. I rested my hammer on a rafter and watched. She pricked at the dried mud here and there, then after a long moment, she jabbed the stick into the soil and left it. Uneasy, I watched her stride back to the house.

This time I had no doubt. The darkness I'd seen earlier seemed to be growing.

Ezra finished the outhouse seat, put all four boys to pulling nails again, then worked with me on the roof.

Each time he climbed the ladder, I saw him searching the streets below for Josiah.

"He'll make it home," I told him more than once.

Ezra always nodded and said, "Yessir," but I knew he wouldn't breathe easy again till he saw his grandson with his own eyes.

I slid a board into place near the corner of the roof and nailed it to the rafters, but I couldn't get Ezra off my mind. I couldn't stop thinking of the shadow I'd glimpsed in his eyes when I'd told him about Josiah. It was easy to see he was worried, but I'd seen something else, too, something I suspected might come from never being master of your own fate. After straining at Papa's leash for so long, that sort of thing wasn't hard for me to recognize, but unlike Ezra and Josiah, I knew my life would change.

By midday, Aunt Julia ran out of fresh water, and before we could eat, she had to send Ezra down the alley with buckets to fetch more. He looked tired, and sweat glistened on his dark skin. He'd been working since before dawn and had made countless trips up and down the ladder, bringing me heavy lumber and slate. I'd have to see that he rested a bit when he came back.

I squinted toward town from my perch on the roof, trying to make out a trace of smoke I'd seen earlier. It was hard to tell its source. At first there'd been only one fire, but now I saw several.

I put down my hammer, ready to quit for a while, and took one last look down the streets. Like Ezra, I'd watched for Josiah all morning, but this time, I thought I saw him walking beside a man pulling a kid's wagon.

I started to yell for Ezra, then remembered he was gone. I blocked the sun with my hand and looked again. It was Josiah all right, and he had Henry with him!

I scrambled down the ladder and up the stairs, yelling for Ella Rose.

"What is it?" Mama asked. "What's happened?"

"Josiah's back," I told her, "and Henry Covington's with him."

Ella Rose stood motionless in the doorway. "Did you say 'Henry'?"

I nodded and laughed. "Come on!" I said, grabbing her hand. We raced down the side stairs while Josiah and Henry rounded the corner off Broadway onto Thirty-fifth.

"Henry!" Ella Rose shouted.

He dropped the handle on his wagon, broke into a run, and swept her off her feet. I stood back, watching, while her skirt and petticoats swirled around his legs.

While they hugged, I helped Josiah push Henry's wagon into the washed-out yard. He let the handle drop and backed away, no doubt aware of the way he smelled. The odor was truly terrible, but the smell of death clinging to him wasn't what bothered me most. It was his eyes. They were full, too full, as if he'd never get shed of what he'd seen. I knew the horror had to be more than any one person should have to carry and wished I could help ease his burden, but I didn't know how. Instead, I found myself pulling away, not wanting him to speak of it, not wanting him to even think of it. Thankfully, his eyes told me he felt the same. It was far too soon for words.

"Oh, Henry," Ella Rose cried. "I thought you were gone." She touched his face, his hair, his shoulders, as if she couldn't quite believe he was there in front of her. "Are your mama and daddy okay? And what about Spencer and Beth and Amanda?" She sucked in a quick breath. "You have to tell me. Tell me everything."

"Slow down, Ella Rose. Slow down. Let's sit there on the steps so we can talk." He tugged her toward the stairs, but she stomped her foot and stood her ground.

"Stop it!" She jerked her hand away, glaring at him. For a moment I saw the same fierce glint in her eyes that I'd seen when Papa reported that he'd found her daddy, but the anger quickly turned to regret.

"I'm sorry," she said. "It's just that your family is all I have now. I need to know."

He gave her a slow nod and pulled in a breath. "It's just me and Spence left, Ella Rose. When the wave hit and the house broke apart, I grabbed Spence and jumped. We lost everyone else in the water, and I haven't seen even one of them since. I've looked everywhere."

She wrapped her arms around him and sobbed into his shoulder. "Your sweet mama and daddy. Beth and little Amanda. I'm so sorry, Henry." She looked up at him, her cheeks wet with tears. "My daddy's gone, too."

He nodded. "When I ran into Josiah, he told me how things were for you and the Braedens. That's why I brought the food. They're rationing supplies in town today, and Chief Ketchum said I could take a share to all of you here."

She wiped her cheeks with her sleeve and stared at the wagon, eyes suddenly vacant. "It will certainly be welcomed, Henry. Thank you."

For a moment, they said nothing more, sinking toward that dazed and barren place I'd seen so many go when their loss became too sharp to bear. But Ella Rose blinked, like stirring from a dream, and pulled Henry toward the stairs where Josiah and I waited. "Come help get the food to the kitchen," she said, "then you must meet the two Mrs. Braedens. They will be so pleased to see you."

Josiah backed away. "Sorry, miss, but I needs to wash up good 'fore I hep."

She looked at him, eyes soft and knowing, and he quickly lowered his eyes.

"I'll send Andy out with some strong soap and a basin of water for you, Josiah. Clean clothes, too," she said. "Seth and Henry will help get this to the kitchen, and as soon as you're finished washing, you come up and eat. Seth's mama has something good waiting for you in the oven."

He slowly raised his head, but not enough to look her in the eye. "Yes'm, Miss Covington. Thank you, ma'am," he mumbled, and disappeared behind the house.

I stared at Ella Rose, watching her gather tins of sardines and salmon into her apron. Her gentle words to Josiah fluttered inside me, sweet, like the jasmine-scented breeze that swept through my window before the storm.

She smiled at me, and my heart was a sudden maze I couldn't navigate.

Chapter

~ 21 ~

Ezra's eyes had glittered with relief when he saw his grandson. And when I looked at Josiah, it was easy to see that, for him, home had never been the house out back. It had always been his grandfather.

As we walked Henry back downstairs to say good-bye, I wondered if I'd misjudged him those first few days at work. Either that, or the storm had changed his thoughtless ways. Not only had he brought our ration of food to us, but he'd picked up a copy of the Galveston *Daily News* as well, a smaller-than-usual edition printed on a hand press. It provided a long list of the dead, and surprisingly, a short list of the "Not Dead" who had been wrongly reported the day before. Aunt Julia had searched the names intently while we talked, then folded the paper and stuffed it in her apron pocket.

I liked seeing this generous side of Henry, and I guess Aunt Julia was impressed with him, too. Once outside, she smiled her gratitude and invited him to fetch his four-year-old brother and stay with us, but he refused.

"But Henry," Ella Rose argued, "you get on so well with Seth, and Spence would have Kate to play with. Won't you just think about it awhile before you say no?"

He shook his head. "I have a debt to pay, Ella Rose. The Dobsons pulled me and Spence through a window during the storm when I thought we'd drown for sure. Now they need my help to rebuild their house."

She glanced up at him, and though I could see she'd finally accepted his decision, Henry wasn't through. He reached for her hand. "Why don't you come back with me?"

My heart clenched tight at the awful prospect of being without her. I held my breath and waited while she grew still, thinking about his offer.

Finally, she shook her head. "It's the same for me," she said. "The Braedens have been good to me, and I don't want to leave the children."

He nodded. "Then you should stay."

"But you *will* come visit as often as you can, won't you, Henry? And bring Spence?" She wrapped her arms around him. "I couldn't bear it if you didn't."

"I will, I promise."

He slid from her embrace, grabbed the handle on the empty wagon, and glanced back at me. "Can you walk a ways with me, Seth?"

I nodded, curious about the look he'd tossed me. He gave Ella Rose a last wave, and when we were out of earshot, he told me about finding Mr. Farrell tangled in a tree Sunday morning, drowned, about five blocks away from his home.

"If it hadn't been for the gap between his front teeth," Henry said, "I'm not sure I could've recognized him."

I shook my head. It was a great loss. "Mr. Farrell was a good man and a fair boss, and I would've liked working for him again one day."

Henry nodded.

"What about Zach and the rest of the Judsons? Any word of them?"

"They're gone, Seth. Ever' last one of them, along with their house."

The news sank inside me, and for a moment, I felt surprise that Zach's passing had hit me so hard. I didn't really know him. Or his family. But thinking back on it, I knew I'd seen something uncommon in this quiet man from the beginning, something that pulled me in, made me care what happened to him. During those few days of working with him, Zach had probably taught me more about myself and what I wanted in life than anyone. Even Papa. If the Good Lord had a reason for bringing this man into my life, that had to be why.

"You knew about the order to barge the bodies out yesterday and bury them at sea, right?" Henry asked.

"Yeah, they made Josiah go."

"Well, they took them eighteen miles out all right, but even with the weights, hundreds of those bodies washed up on the beach this morning." He glanced up at me. "They're still washing in."

I stopped and stared at him, remembering the fires I'd seen from the rooftop. "They're burning them now, aren't they?"

He nodded. "Workers dug trenches at first, but now they're burning them where they find them, just piling the wreckage on top of them and torching it. It's a terrible sight, Seth, terrible. But with this heat, the bodies are coming apart and there's worry about disease, so what else can they do? With your uncle and cousin still missing, I just thought you'd like to know so you can find a way to tell the women."

Henry looked as sick as I felt. It didn't sit well with either of us knowing that our missing family would most likely help feed those fires. And telling Aunt Julia was something I didn't want to think about, but I nodded all the same. "Thanks, Henry. If there's anything I can do . . ."

He shook his head and shrugged. "There's nothing much any of us can do."

I thanked him again for the food, wished him well, and left him to make his way back to the Dobsons.

After Ezra and Josiah ate and rested a bit, they began work on the veranda while I finished up the roof over Ben's room. Ezra had been told about the fires, but I still didn't know how to tell Aunt Julia what I'd learned. More plumes of smoke dotted the city, and I worried that she might've already seen them from the upstairs windows and figured it out.

I fixed the last shingle to the roof, climbed down the ladder, and went to the kitchen. I found Mama working on Papa's food basket, and in a hushed voice, I asked where Aunt Julia was.

"In the parlor, scraping mud."

I nodded and pulled a chair from the table. "Can you sit for a minute? I've got something I need to tell you."

"What is it?" She wiped her hands and sat down.

"The bodies Josiah helped bury at sea began washing onto the beach this morning."

Her hand flew to her mouth.

"They had to start burning them, Mama. I saw the fires from the roof. Henry said they didn't have a choice." She stared at me till I had to look away. "We might not have to tell the boys yet, but Aunt Julia needs to know."

For a long moment, she said nothing, then she leaned across the table and put her hand on mine. "We'll do it together, right after supper," she whispered.

I nodded and glanced at the basket. "Are you almost through with Papa's meals?"

"Almost. Why?"

"Matt needs to be told, too, before he heads off to the railroad bridge."

Her face crumpled in pain. Like me, she no doubt wished she could protect him from what he'd see, but it was unavoidable. Unless . . .

"Mama," I said, "let *me* take the basket to Papa tonight."

She looked up at me, hopeful, but quickly shook her head. "You're needed here. Matt's old enough to understand, but Seth, please tell him not to speak of it to the rest of the children, won't you? Not yet."

"Yes, ma'am. Just send him to find me before he leaves. I'll be out front, working on the veranda."

I headed for the door and felt Mama's hand on my shoulder. I turned, and she wrapped her arms tight around me.

Aunt Julia's eyes glistened with tears when Mama and I told her what was taking place all over the city, but she quickly gained her composure and dried her eyes. Ezra had been right in his assessment of her. She refused to share her grief, choosing to keep it locked up tight, as if some precious part of Ben and Uncle Nate might fly away if she opened her heart.

When she went upstairs to bed, I crept off to the roof, too full of misery to stay in the house any longer. From thirty feet in the air I saw at least a dozen fires set at intervals along the beach and throughout the city. The sky blazed, and stars disappeared behind an increasingly sick-sweet smoke.

Before long, I heard the ladder rattle against the eaves. Without a word, Josiah joined me on the dark roof, where we sat like ghosts, watching Galveston burn its dead.

Chapter

~ 22 ~

Mama found Sarah Louise's name carved on the board wedged in the magnolia tree. I knew it was bound to happen, but I hadn't wanted to speak of her, hadn't wanted to tell anyone that we'd been forced to leave her in that awful place. Something in Mama's eyes seemed to unlock the words, and like an over-turned glass, the story spilled out of me. Later, I found one of Mama's white paper flowers tacked to the carved board.

Days blurred one into another, filled with repair work and heat from dawn to dusk and marked only by the *Daily News* that Ezra had begun to pick up for us every morning. Aunt Julia and Ella Rose always sat together at the table, head to head, poring over the dead list. Occasionally I'd hear them call out names they knew, or breathe a sigh of relief that a friend they'd searched for wasn't there. Ben and Uncle Nate would never be on the list. None of us could bring ourselves to report them dead. Seeing Aunt Julia's face when she read their names would be more than any of us could bear.

With so little fresh water available, Mama and Aunt Julia had a difficult time clearing the mud away, and tub baths and laundry had become a luxury we couldn't afford. But by Wednesday evening, we heard that the city mains had been opened. Cheers rang throughout the house, even though we knew it might take a few days for clean water to reach Thirty-fifth Street.

To our amazement, Archer, Uncle Nate's horse, ambled into the yard that evening, too. A frayed rope dangled from his neck, and Ezra said that he'd likely been found by the militia and used to pull dead wagons. Archer dropped his nose to the ground, snuffling along the salt-crusty mud, searching for something green. We'd have to see about getting a ration of grain and hay tomorrow.

Andy and Will couldn't keep their hands off him, and even Aunt Julia had to rub his nose and pat his neck. The big brown gelding never moved a muscle, as if he knew he was part of something bigger, part of a rare miracle that might still happen for us. If Archer could make it back, then Ben and Uncle Nate might, too. And maybe even Henry's family.

Aunt Julia seemed to tuck that fragile hope away, and after supper, we celebrated the horse's return by watching the boys work on their tree fort. They hauled scrap lumber into the ash tree's bare limbs and hammered with such gusto even Aunt Julia and Ella Rose had to smile.

On Thursday, the Galveston *Daily News* finally printed a full-sized paper and gave the first accounting of the storm. The telegraph office opened, too, and on Friday, banks were back in business.

The temperature hit a steamy one hundred degrees that same evening. From the veranda roof where I was working, I could see the gulf, green and inviting but deserted except for the fires. Not a single soul dared enter the water, and though we all longed for something other than rationed canned foods, no one would eat from the abundant supply of fish, either. As long as the dead still washed ashore, the gulf would remain an unclean enemy.

Ezra ended up making all the trips into town to pick up our rations, insisting that Josiah and I were needed at home, but I knew there was more to it than that. The army had sent soldiers, and martial law had been declared on Thursday. They brought tents and food with them, which were badly needed with so many homeless, but Ezra still worried that the militia might take us, or worse yet, that his grandson might be mistaken for a looter and shot.

What worried me most was what Josiah had been

forced to do on that barge. He'd already seen enough to haunt his every waking moment, but I'd heard him cry out from nightmares, too. I was thankful Ezra was downstairs, right there beside him to help ease him back into the world of the living.

The steamer *Lawrence* brought a hundred thousand gallons of fresh water to the island, and the *Charlotte Allen* ferried a thousand loaves of bread from Houston. The tug *Juno* went to work, too, carrying provisions and medical workers.

We moved through the days, trying to gain some sense of order in our lives, but we never spoke of the growing number of fires. There had been reports that the dead might reach five thousand. Every day the count seemed to rise as more bodies were found buried under wreckage. I wondered how long the air would smell of death and burnings, how long debris would choke the city, but mostly I wondered how, in such a short time, we'd come to accept these things as almost normal.

Saturday morning, one full week after the storm, Matt came home from the railroad bridge later than usual. His eyes were red and his mood surly. I caught him before he went inside and asked him what was wrong.

"Nothing," he said, heading for the stairs.

I grabbed his arm. "If Mama sees you this way, you'll be answering more questions than mine."

He stared at me a moment, then pulled away. "Okay, okay. I'll tell you." He sucked in a deep breath. "Papa said I had to wake him no later than daybreak, and when I didn't, he swore at me."

I tossed him a sideways glance. "Did you oversleep?"

He shook his head, but pain washed across his face. "Aw, Seth, he's been working so hard—harder than I've ever seen anyone work. I just thought I'd let him sleep a speck longer is all."

"You must've made him really mad. I've never heard Papa use a swear word. Not even once."

"Yeah, well, I have," he muttered.

I laughed. "By this evening he'll have forgotten all about it. You'll see. Now go find the boys. They've been waiting on you to get home so they can finish up the tree fort."

He took off, looking somewhat relieved, and I went around back to put up a new clothesline for Mama and Aunt Julia. Clean water had finally reached us yesterday, and they were up to their elbows in suds, scrubbing the grime from all our clothes and bedding.

"When we're finished with this," Mama said, "I plan to get myself into that tub upstairs and soak for a solid hour."

I smiled but had to admit that after a full week of heat and mud and grime, a tub bath sounded pretty good.

The repair work on the veranda had been going well, but I'd been too busy to see much of Ella Rose. I caught myself checking windows while I worked, watching for her and listening for her voice. I rarely saw her smile anymore and worried that her loss might have become too much for her. Then something else occurred to me. Even though she had every reason to grieve, perhaps it wasn't that at all. Perhaps she'd stopped smiling because I never talked to her anymore. She might be thinking I didn't want to spend time with her. I shook my head. Any fool alive would want to spend time with someone like Ella Rose, but since she'd taken over full care of Kate and Elliott, and since I'd been working more than twelve hours a day, there'd been little opportunity for that. I began to wonder if there ever would be.

I hung the new clothesline and helped Josiah pick out lumber to rebuild the front stairs. Railing had been salvaged from the house next door, which promised to make the job go much faster, but the more I worked, the more I felt the tiresome weight of worry. When the rail bridge was done, Papa would be home again. He'd appraise my work, and I didn't want to even think about what would happen if I didn't measure up. There would be a battle for sure, because I was danged determined to see that my future would be in carpentry.

Ezra came back from town that afternoon with good news. The electric trolleys were still inoperable, but mule cars had begun running on some of the streets. A mule named Lazy Lil would be pulling car number 66 from Market to Twenty-first, then down Broadway and back. We all smiled. Even the smallest sign of life returning to normal was a cause for celebration these days.

"Hey!" Andy shouted. "That means it'll be coming right past *us*."

"That be right," Ezra said, grinning. "Caked mud on them tracks might slow 'er down, but I reckon she be coming down Broadway right quick."

The boys ran down the street to keep watch, and soon we heard shouts and cheers as Lazy Lil pulled her car past Thirty-fifth Street to Fortieth, circled around, and headed back to town.

I shook my head. "You'd think those boys had just seen the Labor Day parade all over again."

They came back about the time Mama stepped onto the stair landing to shake out a small rug. She caught all the satisfied grins and tossed them a suspicious frown. "What's got you boys so happy? You haven't been making mischief, have you?"

They laughed and ran upstairs to share the news about Lazy Lil.

Josiah hammered the last nail into the front staircase just at sundown, and we stepped back into the yard to survey our work. This was the first thing we'd built together, just the two of us, and I guess I was a touch surprised at how well we'd done without Zach. The veranda still needed paint, the water-soaked walls inside the house needed plaster, and windows needed glass, but we'd accomplished a lot in the week since the storm. The rest would have to wait till supplies could be brought in by rail.

Josiah hadn't said much since he'd gotten home from the barge, and I still wasn't sure what to do about it, or if I *should* do anything about it. I'd been careful not to push his thoughts back to those dark places, but I couldn't forget how he'd protected me that day at the morgue, how he'd taken on a task that even grown men had tried to refuse, leaving me free to go home.

He frowned, looking hard at the job we'd just finished, but the corners of his mouth soon lifted. That smile was the first sign I'd seen that maybe a small portion of his gruesome night in the gulf might be behind him.

Satisfied, I walked back to the newly finished stairs with him, and we sat on the bottom step, watching the pink and orange sky turn deep purple. Getting Uncle Nate's house repaired had made me feel that perhaps the world could still be set right, and that maybe, just maybe, there wasn't much Josiah and I couldn't do if we set our minds to it.

"I've been thinking about tomorrow," I said finally. "Thinking we might need to spread out just a bit, see if we can scrounge up more lumber—a lot more." I glanced up at him. "We've got us a house to build, right?"

Josiah hesitated, but only for a moment, then he grinned so wide I had to laugh.

"Yessir," he said, "I reckon we do."

I put my elbows on the step behind me and leaned back, thinking about the look on Ezra's face when we told him he'd soon have his house back. Josiah leaned back, too, and we sat there smiling, shoulder to shoulder, watching the twilight sky till Mama called us in to supper.

Chapter

~ 23 ~

Mama and Aunt Julia stayed busy heating water for hours that evening, and after supper, every male in the house got a tub bath. I leaned back in the soapy water, not wanting to get out, but with all four boys banging on the door, I had no choice but to towel off and make way for them.

"It's about time," Lucas said.

I laughed. "Since when did bathing become your favorite pastime?"

His face puckered in a frown. "Since half the world's mud ended up on Galveston Island."

Later that night, I slid between crisp sheets, fresh off the line, and closed my eyes. If the scent of jasmine could've drifted through the windows right then instead of death and smoke, I might've imagined myself back in my own bed. I thought about Ella Rose lying with Kate in Will's bed, just yards away under Aunt Julia's bedroom windows, and I wondered if she ever lay awake, thinking of me.

The convent bells rang Sunday morning, but out of the dozens of churches in the city, only a few could hold services. Wind and water had swept away steeples, shattered windows, and ripped off roofs. Mama insisted that I read a few verses from the Bible before breakfast. "A little something to think about on God's day," she said, but I was thankful she didn't ask us not to work. With all that needed to be done, it seemed to me that God, above all, would understand.

After breakfast, Josiah and I cobbled together a sled to pull behind Archer and headed out to find usable lumber. Ezra made us promise to stay close by and to be always watchful of the militia, but with so much wreckage around, we didn't have to go far. The hardest part was freeing good boards from the twisted rubble. The boys let loose pitiful groans when we told them we needed more nails, but they went right to work pulling and straightening, and easily kept up with us, attacking each new load of boards as soon as it arrived.

By the end of the day, we'd hauled enough used lumber to give us a good start on the house, but it was clear we'd need lots more. The two-room building would be simple, like before, a little shotgun house sitting four feet off the ground, but if I could manage it, I planned to add a small porch under the back gable, a place where Ezra could sit in the shade and watch his new garden grow.

I glanced at the old vegetable patch, barren and crusted with salt, but I remembered well the tall stalks of okra. A big plate of fried okra would taste mighty good about now. I couldn't recall the last time I'd had something that didn't come out of a can. Rations of flour and lard kept plenty of biscuits and pan bread on the table, but I didn't care if I never saw another tin of salmon or sardines.

I woke before daylight Monday morning and realized that I'd been dreaming of Zach. I'd been working with him again, side by side, drawn into that mystifying current of his. I lay perfectly still, breathing in the wonder of that, trying to hang on to the connection, that simple truth that ran like a river between us. In the end, Zach slipped away.

I finally dressed and went down to breakfast, but even while I ate and spoke with Josiah and Ezra about the house, the dream haunted me, making me feel as if I were caught between two worlds.

After breakfast, Josiah and I began work on the foundation, even though we knew we'd have to put in many more days of gathering lumber to complete the house. When Matt got home, he surprised us by rigging the sled to Archer and marshaling the boys into the job. They even managed to pry four windows loose from the wreckage next door. Ezra cleaned away the bits of broken glass, then headed out with the boys to see what else could be scavenged.

The *Daily News* had been reporting that an average of one hundred bodies a day were being recovered by demolition gangs dismantling the long ridge of debris encircling the city, but on Wednesday, September 19, workers uncovered 273. In the next day's paper, I read, "It is possible, but highly improbable, that the list of storm victims will aggregate six thousand souls."

Six thousand.

The number sank inside me, impossible, and yet I'd seen the miles of houses sitting topsy-turvy, the vast piles of debris strewn across hundreds of acres where better than three thousand homes had once stood. I'd seen the overfull morgues, the loaded barges, the smoke-filled skies.

Maybe six thousand wasn't an impossible number after all.

Later that day, the Hodges family sent word through Ezra that a few stores in town had electric lights now and that Clara Barton, president of the American Red Cross, had arrived to offer aid to Galveston. We heard, too, that important people like Joseph Pulitzer and

William Randolph Hearst were sending help and that contributions had begun arriving from people all over the country. I was thankful, but sometimes I wished we could just leave, get Aunt Julia and Ella Rose away from the massive rubble, the smoke-filled skies, and the aching loss that bled the life right out of them. Mr. Hodges said many had done just that, begging rides on the *Juno,* the *Lawrence*—anything that would float. People gathered at the docks with nothing more than the tattered garments on their backs, and the mainland took them in, fed and clothed them, and opened their homes, hotels, and boardinghouses to them.

But I knew Papa would never leave the island. Even I had come to realize I didn't want to go. The storm that ravaged Galveston had left behind much more than wreckage and mud and death. It had left a challenge.

With all of us working, the salvaging and building went quickly. My dream about Zach stayed with me throughout the steamy days, a reminder of all that was possible, and soon, Josiah and I fell into a rhythm of our own. Words dwindled, no longer needed, and the hot hours passed without notice.

By Thursday evening, we both knew something had changed between us. We set the ridge row on Ezra's house, then climbed down to wash up for supper. I reached for the soap and saw Josiah toss me a curious glance.

"What?" I asked.

He shrugged. "Strange is all."

"Strange?"

He shrugged again. "Onliest time I ever worked like this, it be with Mr. Zach."

I slowly lathered my hands. "Yeah, me too."

Chapter

~ 24 ~

Early Friday morning, I climbed up to the new ridge row to set rafters and looked out over Broadway. The morning sun had cast long shadows across the street, and from one of them, Papa and Matt stepped into view.

"Papa's home!" I shouted at Josiah. "The bridge must be finished." A small part of me sighed with relief, though the resentment he'd stirred in me the day he left Josiah and me at the morgue always bubbled close to the surface. I scrambled back down again, hollered through the screen at Mama, then set off down the road.

Papa's face, scruffy with almost two weeks' growth, looked thinner but happy, and he smiled as soon as he saw me. I hesitated a moment, then finally held out my hand. He grabbed it, pulled me to him, and hugged me hard against his chest.

It startled me. I couldn't remember the last time he'd done something like that. I pulled back, looking at him closely, and felt his weary smile working at the knot in my belly, untangling the bitterness I'd been carrying around with me.

"Tho-mas!" Mama hollered from the stairs.

She hiked her skirt immodestly high and ran down the steps and out into the road. Papa grabbed her up like they were both sixteen again, and Matt laughed out loud.

"Are you home for good?" she asked.

Papa nodded. "The rail bridge is finished, and supply trains will be arriving soon."

Mama's face shone with happiness. She wrapped her arm around his waist, and they turned toward home.

Matt followed behind, grinning.

Once inside, Papa hugged Kate and the boys, one by one, but Andy and Will seemed to hang on to him longer than any of them. I think Aunt Julia found it hard to watch. She quickly turned to the stove, insisting that Papa should have a hot breakfast, but I'd seen the pain in her eyes, that bittersweet look of joy and loss. I saw it in Ella Rose's face, too.

Everyone in the house gathered around the table to watch Papa eat his first hot meal since before the storm. He looked achy-tired and empty, like the bridge had drained him of everything but his smile. Mama pulled Kate from his arms and sat her in the chair next to him, but she climbed right back onto his lap and buried her fingers in his beard. Mama fussed, but he shook his head and slowly ate his grits with one arm wrapped around Kate.

Mama hurried to get a bed ready for Papa. She moved their few things from Aunt Julia's room into Ben's repaired room, but while she was gone, Papa stretched out on the parlor floor to play with Kate and Elliott and fell asleep. Ella Rose quietly pulled the kids upstairs to play, and Mama slipped a pillow under Papa's head.

He was still asleep when Josiah and I came in at noon to eat. I didn't see him again till late that afternoon when I caught him sitting on the ground near the new outhouse, freshly shaved, watching me work.

Seeing him sitting there, so very still, started an anxious flutter inside me. I couldn't tell whether it came from fear or resentment, but I sure felt it, all prickly and worrisome.

Seems I could never tell what Papa was thinking. I tried to see Ezra's house the way he might see it, and while I worked, questions tumbled through my head. Was the ridge row straight? Had I missed checking the crown on a rafter? I glanced at Uncle Nate's house. Had he already looked at the roof? The front stairs?

Josiah pushed a freshly cut rafter up to me. I reached for it but fumbled my grip, and the board crashed to the ground, narrowly missing his shoulder. He gave me a puzzled look, and I cringed, furious with my carelessness. I glanced back toward the outhouse, wondering if Papa had seen, but he was gone.

Relieved, I closed my eyes, pulled in a deep breath, and waited for the flutter to settle. I remembered my dream, that easy, instinctive flow, and as natural as breathing, I looked down just as Josiah pushed the rafter back up to me. I gripped the board, slid it into place, and picked up my hammer.

Josiah and I quickly fell into that invisible rhythm again, and I rode the current, no longer mindful of the worries that Papa's presence had stirred in me. We worked steadily till I noticed that the lumber had taken on sunset hues. Mama would be calling us in to supper soon.

I climbed down the ladder, thinking of Papa again, and saw him sitting at the top of the stairs, bare feet dangling over the back of the landing. I didn't know how long he'd been watching, but I was surprised that I didn't feel the way I had before. Might've been because the work had gone so well, despite my clumsiness, or maybe it was the easy way he swung his feet that made me feel less troubled.

Either way, Papa had helped me learn something about myself, about the fear that seemed to always sleep inside me, and about how quickly it could strangle who I was if I let it. I glanced again toward the house, and when Papa waved, I waved back.

Papa fell asleep again, right after supper, drinking in the night like a man dying of thirst. But on Saturday morning, despite his still weakened appearance, he and Matt started on a small stable for Archer.

Papa didn't say anything to me about the repair work we'd done on Uncle Nate's house, but over the next few days, I did notice something different about him, something thoughtful, almost serene in the way he looked at even simple things. Could've been the sorrow of losing Ben and Uncle Nate the way we did, and all those long days of searching and hoping that made him surrender some of his tightfisted ways. Or maybe it was losing all he owned that had humbled him. Whatever the reason, something had shifted inside him, cracked the tough shell around that tender part of himself he'd always kept locked away. You could see it if you knew what to look for, and I guess I'd been looking for it most all my life.

Now it was there.

A softness in his eyes when he spoke to me, an ear tuned to catch every word, a hand lingering on a shoulder, and to my surprise, the last of my bitterness began to unravel. It was a welcome relief, but even as that darkness slid away, another grew.

Someday soon I'd have to tell Papa my decision about college.

Josiah and I were able to continue building through the next week, thanks to Ezra and the boys. They pulled and straightened nails, took Archer out every day, and brought back enough used lumber and slate to keep us going. Papa worked slow and easy on the stable, but even so, I could see that Matt wasn't cut out for carpentry. He hauled himself into supper every evening like he'd just been released from a chain gang, a sure candidate for college and desk work. While he moaned and groaned, Papa never fussed once. He just grinned.

We finished Ezra's new house that Saturday evening. Josiah and I had made every cut, hammered every nail, and I closed the door behind me feeling good about the work we'd done. But while I washed up, I saw Papa walking all around the place. Slow.

He checked the windows, the roof, looked over the new porch from top to bottom, then disappeared inside.

I felt the flutter start up all over again, mean and fierce, but I held on to my grit. I was determined not to let fear best me this time. I thought of Zach's quiet, abiding strength, the way Josiah and I had plumbed our own depths, tapped our own strengths, and the flutter settled.

My work was clean and precise.

I was a carpenter.

Chapter

25

Right after supper Saturday evening, Ezra spotted a brown hen roosting in the magnolia tree. He hollered for help, and soon every one of us was laughing and chasing that chicken all over the moonlit yard. Before long, Ezra had the thing in a small makeshift pen, and we stood there staring at it, wondering if we should keep it for eggs or Sunday dinner.

Lucas frowned. "I bet we upset her egg-laying something terrible."

I had to agree. Chickens didn't take kindly to being chased after bedtime by a dozen wild humans, but I could tell Lucas didn't like the alternative. He could set a cat's broken leg and doctor bloody gashes, but he never could bear watching something die, even chickens.

"Yeah, it's gonna be a long time before *that* hen lays," Matt said.

Andy and Will glanced at each other. "Chicken and dumplings?" they asked in unison.

We all laughed, but eagerness shone in every smile. With another meal of canned salmon staring us in the face, sentimentality didn't stand a chance.

"Well," Mama said, "one hen won't go far, but if Ezra will get it ready for the pot tomorrow, I guess we'll have chicken and dumplings for our Sunday dinner."

"Yes-s-s-s, ma'am," Ezra said, and everyone cheered.

That night Ezra and Josiah moved their things into the new house. Of course, there wasn't much to move, but Aunt Julia made sure they had bedding and a change of clothes. She gave them a cast-iron skillet and a stew pot as well.

"But I insist that you take your meals with us," she said, "right here around this table until things get better."

Ella Rose, her face dark and tight, stood on the stairs, watching Josiah and Ezra say their good-byes. I couldn't figure her out. She truly looked angry.

I didn't like the idea of her turning that look on me, but I had to know what'd been bothering her. I pulled her out to the dimly lit veranda and sat across from her in a wicker chair. "Ella Rose, it's clear something is wrong." I leaned toward her, my forearms on my knees. "Are you mad at Josiah and Ezra about something?"

Starlight glinted in her eyes. "Why would you think that?"

I shrugged. "Then maybe it's me. Have I done something to offend you?"

She shook her head slowly. "Nothing."

She'd barely whispered the word, but I flinched. I'd felt the sharp edges and knew there'd be more.

"Nothing except have a mother and father, an aunt and cousins, a home and a bed." She tossed me a bitter look. When it slid away, I saw shock, then regret. She blinked and covered her face with her hands, smothering a flood of sobs.

I didn't know what to do. Then I realized that there wasn't much I *could* do. I couldn't bring her family back, her home, her friends. I had nothing to give her.

Except me.

I pulled her to her feet and wrapped my arms around her. "You already have what I have, Ella Rose. Right now, this minute. My father and mother—all my family—they love you like their own."

She wiped away her tears and looked up at me. "And you, Seth?"

I nodded. "And me, too."

She pulled in a deep breath and let it out slow. "Thank you," she whispered, and turned to go inside.

Sunday morning Henry and Spencer surprised us with a visit, and for the first time since the storm, we took a day off from work. Papa disappeared into Uncle Nate's study, Mama put the hen to stewing, and the boys climbed into their tree fort.

More and more, Aunt Julia had been looking after the little ones, and she did so again, urging Ella Rose to sit with me and Henry on the veranda. She insisted we do something fun. "Like you used to," she said, pushing a Parcheesi game into my hands. We gathered outside around a small table and opened up the box, but little Spence didn't want to leave his brother.

"He's been like this since we lost Mama, Papa, and the girls," Henry said. "He just doesn't like to let me out of his sight."

Aunt Julia nodded. "Of course he doesn't." She disappeared inside for a moment, then came back with paper and glue. "We'll sit right here on the floor by the door so he can see you, and we'll make paper chains to decorate the dining room for our big dinner."

Kate clapped her hands, and with a little encouragement, Spence was soon smiling at Henry through the screen door.

I hadn't seen Ella Rose this happy since before the storm, and I was finding it difficult to keep from staring at her. I thought about how we'd looked forward to swimming that weekend of the storm, how I'd hoped to take her dancing at the Garten Verein one day, and I wondered if she ever thought of me like that. After last night, I was afraid she might be thinking of me as the brother she never had. If so, I wasn't sure a notion like that could be changed.

But even that grim worry couldn't mar the day for long. We talked and laughed and played Parcheesi while the aroma of stewing chicken drifted from the kitchen. The veranda soon became my own private ship, and for a while, the three of us sailed away, far from the never-ending fires, the splintered homes, and the aching loss, till all I could see was the deep blue of Ella Rose's eyes.

Chapter

26

October swept in, bringing more change and, occasionally, cooler days. Trees stood bare, salt still encrusted every inch of earth, but big loaves of Mama's yeasty bread finally graced the table at every meal.

Though fires continued to burn, the sound of hammers and saws, axes and crowbars, could be heard everywhere, eating away at the twisted wreckage, exposing usable lumber, sinks, commodes, and always, more dead souls. Wagons and buggies now rumbled along many streets without hindrance, and trains puffed into the city daily with carloads of supplies and workers.

Besides the endless dead list, the *Daily News* now advertised brooms, shovels, nails, and coffeepots. Want ads asked for carpenters, tinners, bricklayers, and cooks. Lost-item ads listed a missing three-story chicken coop made of iron spokes and wood, and a dairy herd of 150 cows and calves, all swept away in the storm. And then there were personal ads, like the one that stated simply,

"Fred Heidenreich, if alive, come to Twenty-fourth and Church. Your brother is there."

Aunt Julia searched each paper, read every word, then folded it and placed it in a box with the others.

We spent the first half of October plastering walls and painting, then turned to helping the work gangs remove the debris all around us. I think it did Aunt Julia's heart good to see the wreckage finally cleared away, but my long days of working were fast coming to an end. Public schools would open soon, thanks to donations and volunteer workers.

The *Daily News* announced that high-school students needed to report on October 22 to the campus known as K School on Avenue K till repairs to Ball High School could be finished. Central High, Josiah's school, had been wrecked, too, but he'd left last year with no plans to return. After the death of his mother this past winter, his wages had been needed to help support himself and Ezra.

It seemed odd to think about school again after all we'd been through, and for a short while, I let myself daydream about the possibility of not returning at all. Debris-filled lots were being cleared all over town, making way for the thousands of new homes and businesses that were needed, so I knew I could get work. Papa had done so easily. Josiah had, too, and I could tell that, like me, he'd discovered a satisfaction in his labor not every man finds. But I decided not to speak of these things to Papa just yet. Long before our lives changed, I'd made him a promise to finish school, and I would stand by my word.

Just days before school started, Ella Rose stated firmly that, although her father had left her an adequate inheritance, she would not be returning to Ursuline Academy. She looked at me and smiled. "I'll be attending public school."

I saw Papa open his mouth, no doubt wanting to remind her that she should consider what her father had wanted, but he didn't speak.

It surprised me.

Aunt Julia's face puckered with concern. She'd come to depend upon Ella Rose for much more than help with Elliott. "You'll still remain here with us, won't you?" she asked.

Ella Rose nodded. "For as long as you'll have me."

Aunt Julia's fear faded, and she smiled.

I smiled, too, but not just for her happiness. I saw my last year of school unfolding in front of me, full of morning and evening walks with Ella Rose, and the sting of returning to school disappeared.

Chapter

27

Starting any new school would've been difficult, but it was especially so in Galveston. Back home in Lampasas, halls had always rung with shouts and laughter the first day. Students crowded around bulletin boards to see what room they'd been assigned, to exchange gossip, and to talk about what the new year would bring, but I heard no laughter in the halls of K School. Only questions.

"Where's Sylvia Langdon?" someone asked.

"Have you seen Jess Bulloch?"

"Where are the Sutter kids?"

But even worse were the quiet replies.

"Sorry, no one's seen her."

"Jess's family died in the storm, so he went to live with an uncle on the mainland."

"Sutters? They drowned. All of them."

Clothing had been scarce since the storm. Many

students were barefoot, wearing whatever had been donated or salvaged from debris and the hundreds of mud-soaked trunks scattered throughout the city.

Desks sat empty in every room, but it wasn't till later that day that we heard how many. Better than 25 percent of the city's student body was missing. Seems the storm had been hardest on the young.

I got through those first hours like everyone else, and when the day was finally over, I walked home with Ella Rose. She looked pale, almost sick, and I knew it was because she'd discovered more friends missing. I wondered how many but didn't ask. Instead I rambled on about teachers and books and reading assignments, when all I could think about was how much I wanted to see her smile again.

Over the next few weeks, school days leveled out, and I finally heard laughter in the halls. Dwelling on history and literature instead of loss might've had something to do with it, but I figured cleaner air probably had a hand in it, too. The searing smoke rarely darkened the sky during the day anymore, nor did it block the millions of stars at night. In its place I finally smelled new lumber, horses and hay, and clean gulf breezes. Shipments of fresh food replenished the markets, too, and Mama splurged on eggs and bacon, squash and greens, apples and pears.

Slowly, we turned toward the way life used to be. I began thinking about the best time to tell Papa my decision concerning college while Aunt Julia and Ella Rose practiced calligraphy, poring over pages of scrolled and feathered script, looking more like mother and daughter than friends. Telephones rang again, electric lights shone from every window, and outside, Galveston's streets were finally clean. The city gathered around Thanksgiving tables, and moved on to trim Christmas trees and sing carols, but every eye reflected pain. The deepest wounds, the ones unseen, still festered.

I think the holidays were hardest of all on Aunt Julia, though she tried to hide it. There'd been no graves for her to visit, no final words and prayers, and especially no solace from knowing how life had ended for her husband and son. Ella Rose seemed to have finally made peace with her loss, and Andy and Will, like most young boys, were easily distracted from theirs. Yet, in quiet moments, I saw the sorrow and wondered how long our hearts would yearn for healing.

I turned seventeen just before the end of the year. Celebrating the holidays had been difficult enough without squeezing a birthday into it, so I asked Mama not to make a fuss. She nodded, but that night there was fried chicken and apple pie on the table, two of my favorites, and when supper was over, Ella Rose pulled me outside into the crisp-still night.

Streetlights cast yellow circles down the block toward the gulf, and oyster shells crunched under our feet. "Where are we going?" I asked.

She tossed me a mysterious smile. "You'll see."

"You know, don't you?"

"What? That you're seventeen today and you didn't want cake and presents?"

I laughed. "Well, yeah. How did you know?"

"Ben told me right after you moved here. He said you were exactly one year and ten days younger than he was."

"So you figured it out?"

She nodded. "But your mother said we weren't supposed to mention it, so I planned a little surprise of my own."

"A surprise?"

She held a finger to her lips. "Soon," she said.

In the distance, I saw the electric glow from the repaired Garten Verein. She grabbed my hand, pulled me into a run, then collapsed on a bench near the pavilion. Like that first night here with Ben, band music drifted out to us, mingling with the soft sounds of surf.

"It's beautiful, isn't it?" she asked, still breathless from our run. "It's almost like it was before."

I nodded, but it was her cold-blushed cheeks I saw, not the pavilion. Her warm breath puffed into the chill air, and her hair fanned around her shoulders, golden against the dark wool of her coat. With more than a little effort, I pulled my attention back to the pavilion. "So why are we here?" I asked.

"Because everyone should have music and bright lights on their birthday." She reached into her pocket and pulled out a small box. "And because I wanted to give you this when we were alone."

All smiles, she pushed the box into my hand and squirmed on the bench beside me, waiting.

I stared at the bright red ribbon.

"Well, aren't you going to open it?"

I laughed, untied the bow, and lifted the lid. Mr. Covington's gold rose tiepin, the one Papa had returned to her the day after the storm, lay shining on white satin. I opened my mouth to tell her it was too much, that I couldn't possibly keep something so precious to her, but the words wouldn't come.

"Daddy bought it shortly after I was born," she said.

"But . . . but, Ella Rose, you have so little left of your father's . . ."

She closed my hand over the pin and smiled up at

me. "He said the gold rose always reminded him of me, and that's exactly why I want you to have it."

That night as I lay in bed, I didn't have to wonder anymore if Ella Rose ever thought of me. She did, and someday there would be more. I'd seen it in her eyes.

Chapter
~ 28 ~

I woke early on New Year's Eve, thinking of college. My decision hadn't changed over the months, but the worry of telling Papa reared its head daily now. I didn't fret any longer that he might disagree with me—he surely would—but I wasn't looking forward to seeing the disappointment in his face. In fact, there wasn't much I wouldn't do to steer clear of that outcome, short of going to college, but for the life of me, I couldn't figure out a way to avoid it.

I'd have to tell him, and it might as well be tomorrow. His disappointment was just something we'd both have to bear.

I dressed, went down for breakfast, and caught Mama alone in the kitchen with Kate. I told her of my plans for the next day, and she nodded, not at all ruffled by the news. She just continued breaking eggs into her mixing bowl as if she'd known all along that this moment was coming.

I stared at her, wondering all over again about the message Papa had me deliver that day he'd chosen to work on the rail bridge. It meant nothing to me at the time, but it must've meant something to Mama. She'd smiled and kissed me on the cheek, like she and Papa shared some great secret. She hadn't even been angry at him for leaving the family with just me to get us through the first weeks following the storm.

I found the whole thing strange.

One by one, the boys ambled in and fell into chairs, sleepy-eyed but happy that there'd be no school today. Kate squirmed, then whined to Mama that she had to go to the outhouse. I saw Mama glance at her skillet of eggs, still cooking, and I knew what was coming. To my surprise, it wasn't my name she called.

"Take her for me, won't you, Matt? She's still so afraid of the bugs."

A look of pure horror flashed across his face as he realized that this particular burden had just been passed to him. He groaned but rose from his chair and took Kate's hand.

I stifled a grin while Mama brought the skillet to the table and spooned eggs onto my plate, but when she flashed a big smile at me, I couldn't hold it any longer. I busted out laughing.

"What's so funny?" Andy asked.

"Yeah," Will said. "What's so funny?"

Lucas tossed me a knowing glance, but he wasn't smiling. I guess he'd already figured out that he, too, might be called upon any day now.

That evening, I told myself that we were gathering along the beach to welcome in the New Year and watch the fireworks, but I think we all knew there was far more to it than that.

People arrived, bundled in coats and hoods, cuddling babies, and holding the hands of small children. Excitement crackled through the crowds, and soon rockets exploded over the water.

Kate and Elliott squealed. Faces around us reflected bright bursts of blue and red and gold, and for a short while, I guess we all lost ourselves in the glittering sky.

When the last spark disappeared, groans of disappointment swept through the gathering, but soon a voice rang out. Then another. And dozens more. We all joined in, and "Auld Lang Syne" swelled in my chest and rose above us, filling the sky, drifting out over the water till the last mellow tone died away. When it was done, we were left standing, arm in arm, before the black gulf.

The crowd grew silent.

I listened to the rhythmic shush of surf while cold salt air bit at my cheeks and memories of the last four months swept over me.

All around, families reached for one another, drawing close. I grasped Ella Rose's hand, and the truer purpose for our gathering rolled toward us as sure as the waves that fell upon the beach.

It was time for good-byes, time to let loose the storm's bindings, but I didn't see how I'd ever be free of the ghosts.

I felt them often, just as I did now, close beside me, expectant, whispering around my ears, fingering through the images in my head. They turned from the beach with me that night, walked beside me along the oyster-shell road, and followed me right through the front door and into my bedroom. Even after the house was hushed with sleep, I could still sense them, sitting in shadowy corners, lingering near the windows, waiting.

I finally slipped out of bed, headed outside, and followed the road till my shoes sank into soft sand. The chill north wind swept through my hair and blew my coat collar up against my neck, but I kept walking.

When I reached the hard wet beach, I stopped a few feet from the foam that snaked along the water and looked out over the gulf. Dark waves carried the moon's silver light toward me like fallen stars, but as I expected, more ghosts came with them.

This time I surrendered, and they quickly pushed through everything in my head. Instead of the beach, I saw Uncle Nate offering me my first carpenter job and laughing at my surprise. I saw Ben leaning over the veranda railing, full of sly smiles, telling me about Ella Rose.

I felt Mr. Covington's handshake and watched a grinning Toby throw his ball. Once more my heart mourned for the young nun and her nine small charges and raced after the woman and child swept down the alley behind Butcher Miller's house.

I grieved again with Captain Munn and Aunt Julia, Ella Rose and Henry, and sent my gratitude to Zach and Mr. Farrell. I asked blessings for the girl in blue gingham, the twin boys, the woman and the sad lost man who helped bury her, and the countless souls finally given up to funeral pyres. Then I whispered Sarah Louise's name, picturing it carried in the wind across Galveston, to the mainland, and into every ear.

I embraced them all, for I could do nothing else, then I tried to put this haunted piece of myself to rest.

It was time to move on, but as I glanced out over the gulf, I knew I'd never be truly free. Dark water would always carry ghosts to me. I'd feel Zach beside me with every nail I hammered; I'd see Toby's grin in every baseball. Blue gingham, washboards, saws, broken mirrors—these things and more would forever speak to me, and I'd listen. I'd remember.

Wind whistled around my ears.

The ghosts had finally grown silent.

I left the dark gulf behind me, and as I walked back across the soft sand toward home, the scent of fresh cut lumber turned my thoughts to the future.

Galveston stretched before me, and on every block, I saw the pale bones of another new house shining under yellow streetlights. Someday soon I'd be there among them.

And tomorrow, Papa would know.

Chapter

~ 29 ~

I woke New Year's Day from another dream about Zach. I'd had several dreams of him since the first, and he never spoke in any of them. We simply worked together, shoulder to shoulder. Somehow these quiet dreams of Zach had helped me get to the heart of who I was. They'd helped me carve away what I no longer needed, sand the rough parts clean and smooth. Now all I thought about was how much I wanted Papa to see what I'd become.

On this particular morning I lay in bed, trying to look at Papa the way Zach might have, trying to choose the words he would've chosen. In the end, it was me who rose from the bed; it was me who asked to speak to Papa in Uncle Nate's study.

A special dinner was in the works for this first day of the year, and the whole house bustled with activity. Aunt Julia had sent Ezra for extra ice, and Mama's baking filled the house with the warm aroma of apples and cinnamon. I just hoped that what I had to tell Papa wouldn't ruin our fine dinner.

It was a strange feeling following Papa from the parlor into the study. I watched him sit in Uncle Nate's chair and seemed to watch myself be seated as well, as if a part of me hung back near the doorway, unwilling to enter. I'm not sure what was said at that point—polite wishes from Papa for a happier New Year, I think—but I do remember that shortly after, I emptied my heart and my words hung in the air between us.

"There will be no college for me, Papa," I told him. "I'm a carpenter, and I can be nothing else."

He stared at me, and I watched for the hard, whittled look that always came when he was displeased, the look that would tell me everything.

But it didn't come.

Instead he rose from his seat and called for Aunt Julia. When she arrived, he whispered something to her, then closed the door and walked slowly to the window.

Uncle Nate's clock ticked on his desk, a north wind whipped bare branches against the glass, and all my old fears and resentments—all that I thought I'd conquered—rushed toward me like a runaway train.

As usual, I couldn't tell at all what Papa was thinking. He hadn't shouted, hadn't insisted. He hadn't even asked me to leave. He'd only turned his back on me and left me waiting, tangled in the web of his silence.

A light rapping turned him around, and he crossed the room to answer it. He pulled the door wide, and in tramped every soul in the house, Ezra and Josiah, too.

Surprise jerked me to my feet. I watched, confused, while Aunt Julia and Ella Rose carried a large, cloth-draped rectangle into the room.

As soon as they'd all taken places around Uncle Nate's desk and turned to face me, Papa cleared his throat. He spoke slowly at first, deliberately and without a smile.

"We'd planned to give you this after graduation, *but* as your mother continually reminds me, the good Lord has a reason for everything."

His eyes twinkled, and to my surprise his mouth stretched into a sudden wide grin.

"And even a fool can tell what that is if he'll just listen." He laughed and pulled away the cloth.

I sucked in a breath and tossed a shocked look at Ella Rose and Aunt Julia. It was their bold and feathered script that graced the shiny black-and-white sign.

Braeden and Son

Building Contractors

I blinked at the words. I hadn't once thought . . . hadn't once dared . . .

Kate and Elliott clapped like they'd just seen another fireworks display, and Aunt Julia's and Ella Rose's eyes glistened with tears.

I turned to Mama. Her cheeks were wet, too, and I finally realized what she must've known all along. Papa had already planned this day when he chose to work on that rail bridge. He'd done it for me, and all this time, Mama had never said a word. She just stood back and let me learn how to walk in Papa's shoes.

I looked at Matt and Lucas, Andy and Will, Ezra and Josiah, and every one of them grinned so wide all I could see was teeth.

But it was Papa's smile that made my heart leap.

I glanced at him, still full of questions, and saw nothing but answers in his face.

Galveston is fast becoming the New York City of Texas. . . .

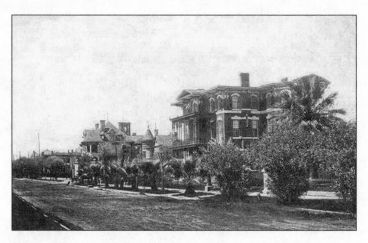

Author's Note

Several years ago my husband came home from work with an old book in his hands. "You have to read this," he said. "It's a full account of the 1900 Galveston Storm, written right after it happened."

Like most everyone in Texas, I'd heard of the hurricane that devastated Galveston all my life and I'd read many articles about it through the years, but this book was different. It had been written while wounds were still tender, while wind and floodwaters still haunted dreams. I opened the century-old frayed cover, and on the first yellowed page, written in faded pencil, was a simply worded inscription as old as the book itself. "In fond remembrance . . ." it began, and from that moment, I was spellbound.

I then read dozens of volumes that related not only the horrific damage this great storm wrought but personal accounts of survival and loss so vivid, so achingly painful, I felt as though I'd experienced it myself.

What might lay beneath this rubble? How many souls?

It was this intimate window to the past that brought me to write *Dark Water Rising,* and in so doing, I wanted to honor some of the personal details that have been recorded. Among the many documented accounts of the Galveston Storm that I drew from, a grown-up Katherine Vedder related the successful efforts of her mother in saving the Longineaus' baby, Tom. She also told how Captain Munn was found naked the next morning with only a mattress ticking to cover him, and how she'd once been the envy of their neighborhood because she'd been allowed to play funeral with her father's hearse and his old mule, Whiskers. Her account provided me glimpses of real people such as the lost Peek family, the grateful Private Billings, the Collums with their parrots and cats, and the Masons with their last surviving tin of sardines and bottle of beer. Much of the dialogue attributed to them was either direct quotes or inspired by Katherine's statements.

Galveston, a small barrier island off the coast of Texas, has a long and colorful history of cannibalistic Karankawa Indians, pirates and buried treasure, Civil War battles, and spirited entrepreneurs. It is only thirty miles long and two and a half miles wide at its greatest point, but at the turn of the century it was one of the largest shipping ports in the United States, second only to New York. The city's future was bright then, but after the historic Saturday of September 8, 1900, its path would be forever altered.

More than 3,600 homes and businesses were destroyed by the Galveston Storm, and 1,500 acres of

From one end of the wharf to the other, sailboats and tugs lay sunk or in jumbled confusion.

coastland swept into the Gulf of Mexico. Among the countless financial losses, fifty thousand bales of cotton, worth more than $3 million, and better than ten thousand head of cattle never saw the market. The city was devastated, but the greatest loss, borne by every single person on the island, was more personal. Children were missing; they and thousands of mothers and fathers, brothers and sisters, friends and neighbors, had been drowned by floodwaters, struck by airborne debris, swept to sea, or trapped in collapsing homes.

Hundreds of boxcars tumbled this way and that, their valuable loads of flour, grain, and cotton ruined.

"If the bodies aren't moved by sundown, they'll have to take them out in pieces tomorrow. So they're barging them eighteen miles out . . . and giving them to the sea."

The official death count hovers at eight thousand—six thousand lost in Galveston and two thousand on the mainland—but the actual figure can never be known. Historians insist that twelve thousand is more accurate, pointing to the many who quickly left the island without reporting missing family members, and to the families who were washed out to sea, leaving no one alive to do the reporting. Then there were some, like the Braedens, who had no bodies to bury and found themselves unwilling to give up hope and report their loved ones dead.

By daybreak Sunday morning, September 9, 1900, even as families all over Galveston waded from damaged

Houses and buildings left standing . . . tilted crazily, and many lay tumbled topsy-turvy, kicked over like toy blocks.

homes for their first glimpse of the ravaged city, the mighty storm continued its destructive, two-hundred-mile-wide path, devastating dozens of Texas towns and sweeping into Oklahoma, Kansas, Iowa, and beyond. Six loggers were killed on the Eau Claire River in Wisconsin. Hurricane-force winds lashed Chicago and Buffalo, downing telegraph lines and halting communication across the whole Midwest.

The storm moved across Michigan and the Canadian

province of Ontario, destroying a million-dollar fruit crop ready for harvest, then sent the steamer *John B. Lyon* and the schooner *Dundee* to the bottom of Lake Erie, along with thirteen men.

By the twelfth of September, four full days after Galveston's destruction, the storm gained strength again as it approached the Canadian Maritime Provinces. Prince Edward Island reported eight small fishing schooners and thirty-eight men lost, and off Newfoundland,

Everywhere we looked, we saw men . . . picking up bodies.

The storm that ravaged Galveston had left behind much more
than wreckage and mud and death. It had left a challenge.

eighty-two schooners were sunk or driven ashore,
another hundred damaged, and seventy-five men were
missing. The fishing fleet of Saint-Pierre et Miquelon
lost nine schooners and 120 men, leaving fifty children
without fathers.

On September 13, the mighty storm finally surged
northeastward across the North Atlantic Ocean, curved
over the top of the world, and is believed to have disappeared above Siberia.

Back in Galveston, not a single life or business had been left unchanged, but even before the dead were at rest, men gathered in storm-damaged buildings to discuss how to rebuild their great city and find a way to prevent such devastation from happening again.

A proposal to erect a seawall was soon drafted and submitted to the state legislature, and on September 19, 1902, work began. Along six miles of beach, men pounded creosoted pilings forty feet into the sand and formed a concrete barricade sixteen feet thick at the base and seventeen feet above mean low tide. This wall stood behind a barrier of granite boulders that extended twenty-seven feet toward the gulf.

The seawall was completed on July 29, 1904, but that wasn't enough for the citizens of Galveston. They wanted the city raised to prevent the massive flooding that had taken so many lives, and each property owner agreed to bear a share of the cost. Soon streetcar tracks, fireplugs, water lines, and even trees and shrubs were removed. One by one, more than 2,100 homes, churches, and businesses were jacked up, some as high as thirteen feet, and sand sucked from the floor of the gulf was pumped onto the island to fill in under all the buildings, covering up roads and grass and flowers. During the eight years it took to raise five hundred city blocks, residents were forced to use long wooden walkways to get to their homes and through town. They suffered immense inconvenience, but with memories of the storm still fresh, there were no complaints. The raising was finished during the summer of 1910, and at last Galvestonians breathed easier.

Since then, the seawall has been extended six times and now covers one-third of Galveston's gulf beaches, and yet the shadow of the Great Storm remains. You can glimpse it in the historic homes and smell it in their tangled gardens of jasmine and magnolia. You can taste it in the salty gulf breezes and hear it, unfailingly, in the rhythmic rush of waves.

It was time to move on . . .

On September 8, 2000, the city gathered for a centennial tribute to the victims of the Galveston Storm, a ceremony that had been two years in the making.

"Hurricanes haunt," said Texas native Dan Rather, keynote speaker and now-retired news anchor. "Galveston will never forget what happened here."

Nor will I.

Marian Hale

ROCKPORT, TEXAS
SEPTEMBER 2006

Acknowledgments

Heartfelt appreciation to my talented writing friends Barton Hill, Julie Hannah, Woody Davis, Kay Butzin, and Heather Miller; to my generous and exceptional editor, Reka Simonsen; my treasured and resourceful parents, June and Robert Freeze; my most ingenious adviser, Wendel Hale; my bright and shining children, Allison, Micah, and especially Aliisa, for candid feedback, invaluable suggestions, and unshakable support; and always to the Rockport Writers Group for their magnificent cheers.

And my deepest gratitude to Katherine Vedder Pauls and all the survivors of the 1900 Galveston Storm for providing windows into their enormous personal loss and Herculean efforts to rebuild the great city of Galveston.